Good Puppy

I went over and took a peek into the kennel, which was huge and spotlessly clean. It was empty.

"Doggy must be inside," I murmured to myself.

Pulling out the key Darity had given me, I hurried around to the front door. The key slid in easily. I pushed the door open and stepped inside.

"RRRROWR!"

A mass of fur and sharp teeth leaped at me. Before I could react, I was pinned to a wall by a hundred pounds of snarling German shepherd.

THE HARDY BOYS

Undercover Brothers®

Available from Simon & Schuster

THE HARDY BOYS

Undercover Brothers®

FRANKLIN W. DIXON

#31 Killer Mission

BOOK ONE IN THE KILLER MYSTERY TRILOGY

Aladdin

New York   London   Toronto   Sydney

ALADDIN
An imprint of Simon & Schuster Children's Publishing Division
1230 Avenue of the Americas, New York, NY 10020
First Aladdin paperback edition November 2009
Copyright © 2009 by Simon & Schuster, Inc.
All rights reserved, including the right of reproduction
in whole or in part in any form.
THE HARDY BOYS MYSTERY STORIES is a trademark of
Simon & Schuster, Inc.
HARDY BOYS UNDERCOVER BROTHERS and related logo are
registered trademarks of Simon & Schuster, Inc.
ALADDIN is a trademark of Simon & Schuster, Inc., and related logo is a
registered trademark of Simon & Schuster, Inc.
For information about special discounts for bulk purchases,
please contact Simon & Schuster Special Sales at 1-866-506-1949
or business@simonandschuster.com.
The Simon & Schuster Speakers Bureau can bring authors
to your live event. For more information or to book an event contact
the Simon & Schuster Speakers Bureau at 1-866-248-3049
or visit our website at www.simonspeakers.com.
Designed by Sammy Yuen Jr.
The text of this book was set in Aldine 401 BT.
Manufactured in the United States of America
10 9 8 7 6 5 4 3 2 1
Library of Congress Control Number 2009929789
ISBN 978-1-4169-8695-9
ISBN 978-1-4169-9706-1 (eBook)

TABLE OF CONTENTS

For the Birds

I am *so* not a cat person.

Okay, that's not fair. Some cats I like. The cute, cuddly ones.

The huge, snarling, striped ones? Not so much. I was starkly reminded of that fact as I faced down three enormous, snarling tigers.

That's right, tigers. As in, six-hundred-pound killing machines.

I shot a look over my shoulder. The iron-barred door leading out of the tigers' enclosure was slightly ajar. That was my escape route. I just hoped the tigers didn't notice it. The last thing my brother Frank and I needed was to be responsible for three loose tigers terrorizing the Bayport Zoo.

One of the tigers let out a low growl. That snapped my full attention back to them.

"Good kitty kitties," I said in what I hoped was a soothing voice.

"Quit kidding around, Joe," Frank hissed from beside me.

He didn't take his eyes off the largest of the three big cats. It was eyeing a chunk of raw meat lying between itself and us. The meat was thick and juicy, oozing with blood.

"I'm not kidding around," I hissed back. "If we don't get that meat before Tigger there decides to have a snack . . ."

"I know. Our only solid piece of evidence goes bye-bye." Frank looked grim. "And those smugglers can keep right on pushing drugs into the hands of local schoolkids."

Frank's a sucker for innocent schoolkids. So am I, actually. That's one of the reasons the two of us joined ATAC. You know—righting wrongs, fighting injustices, keeping illegal drugs out of the hands of schoolkids—that sort of thing.

What's ATAC? I'll get to that in a minute. First, back to the tigers.

"Try to distract them," I whispered to Frank. "Then I'll run in and grab that meat."

"Distract them?" Frank looked at me. "How?

By acting like an even bigger, juicier steak? Anyway, if you make any sudden moves, Shere Khan there will pounce."

"Who?"

He rolled his eyes. "Hello? *Jungle Book*? Ring any bells?"

I decided to ignore that. It didn't seem like the best moment to start discussing movies. "Go back outside and bang on the bars of the cage or something. See if you can get them away from the meat."

Frank looked doubtful. But he did as I said. Sidling back to the exit, he jumped out.

That left me alone with the tigers. Did you ever see a tiger up close and personal? If not, let me tell you: They're huge. *Really* huge.

"Easy, big guys," I singsonged. "Nothing to see here."

I glanced at Frank. Then back at the largest tiger. He looked hungry.

Outside the cage, Frank was doing his part. "Hey!" he called out, rapping on the metal bars with his keys. "Tony the Tiger! Over here!"

Two of the tigers turned to look at him. But the big one kept right on staring at me. Only a twitch of its huge fuzzy ear showed that it had even heard Frank.

Then it licked its chops. Nice. If life was a Bugs Bunny cartoon, I would've transformed into an eight-course meal.

"Good puddy tat," I babbled. "Nice tiger. Those stripes look good on you, did anyone ever tell you that? Very, uh, slimming."

The tiger narrowed its eyes. Maybe it didn't want to be slim.

"You'd better get out of there," Frank called, sounding nervous. "I don't think this is going to—"

CLANG!

The rest of his comment was drowned out by the sound of the cage door slamming shut. "Hey!" I blurted out, jumping and spinning around.

A skinny little guy with greasy hair grinned evilly from the other side of the door. "Time for lunch, boys," he sneered before turning and racing away.

"Go after him!" I yelled to Frank.

He was already grabbing at the door to the cage. But it was no use. When Frank shook it, it didn't budge. The lock had latched automatically when that smuggler slammed it shut.

"But you—," he began.

"GO!" I shouted.

Frank hesitated only for a second. Then he

raced after Greasy Hair. I guess the bad guy hadn't gotten very far, because a moment later I heard an "Oof!" and then a bunch of cursing.

But I wasn't focused on that. The big tiger had just taken a step closer.

"Easy, big guy," I said. I have a pretty cool head in most situations. I can handle just about anything a bad guy can throw at me. But tigers? This was a whole new deal. And I didn't like it.

"Rajah! No!" a female voice cried from somewhere at the back of the enclosure.

That finally got the tiger's attention off me. It pricked its ears, and its head swiveled toward the voice. The other two tigers looked that way too.

I followed their gaze. A girl was standing in an open doorway at the back of the enclosure. Even in my current state of near panic, I couldn't help but notice how pretty she was.

The tigers must have liked the looks of her too. Or maybe they just thought she was bringing more food. They all turned away from me and walked toward her.

I darted forward and grabbed that chunk of meat. It was cool and moist and heavier than I expected. It slimed through my hands and almost slid out of my grip, so I hugged it to my chest. Gross. Now *I* was moist and slimy.

But I didn't stop to worry about that. I ran for that back door, pushing past Zookeeper Babe.

"Are you okay?" she demanded. "And where's your brother? He's not still in there, is he? Oh God . . ."

Okay, that was a little annoying. I mean, sure, I was grateful that she'd just pretty much saved my life and all. But why did cute girls always go for Mr. Tall Dork and Handsome?

"Frank's fine," I said, adjusting my grip on the slippery meat. "Now help me wrap up this steak. The cops are going to want to test the residue inside it right away."

"I hope Mom and Aunt Trudy don't notice that you're coming home wearing a different shirt than you left with," Frank fretted as we parked our motorcycles in the driveway.

I glanced down at myself. I'd tossed the shirt that got slimed by that raw meat back at the zoo. This new one was from the gift shop. I'd had to turn it inside out to hide the embroidered panda cub on the pocket.

"Chill," I advised Frank. "It's not like they wouldn't have noticed if I came home with my shirt coated in blood."

He still looked anxious. That was typical. Frank's

always looking for the worst-case scenario. Me? I prefer not to worry until I have to.

"Anyway," I went on, "I'm glad we finally nabbed those drug smugglers. That was a tough case. Let's hope ATAC gives us a little time off as a reward. I'm ready to relax for a while."

That brings us back to ATAC. The name stands for American Teens Against Crime. It's an undercover crime-fighting group started by our dad, Fenton Hardy, and staffed by teen agents.

Why teens? Simple. We can go certain places and do certain things that adult agents can't pull off. For instance, we were able to pose as high school interns at the zoo and figure out how the drug runners were slipping their merchandise past the cops. Other assignments might send us somewhere like a rock concert or a skateboard park. Basically, anywhere teens would hang out and adults would stand out.

It's pretty much the coolest job in the world.

Nobody was around when we let ourselves into the house. That gave me a chance to sneak upstairs and change my shirt. Better safe than sorry.

Good thing. Because as soon as we flopped on the couch in the den to start relaxing, Aunt Trudy found us. And she had that look in her eye.

Aunt Trudy is Dad's sister who lives with us.

She never got married or had kids, so I guess Frank and I became her substitute kids. She loves to boss us around.

"Where have you two been all day?" she snapped, looking us up and down. Whew! No way that panda shirt would've passed without notice. Not even turned inside out.

Frank and I traded a look. We weren't about to tell her we'd been tussling with tigers at the zoo. But she hates when we just say "around" or something like that. Luckily, our ATAC training has taught us how to think on our feet.

"We were at the library," Frank said. "School project."

She looked unimpressed. "I see. Well, *I* have a project for you, and you'd better snap to it. That clever bird of yours needs his cages cleaned."

I winced and glanced at the big wire cage in one corner of the den. "That clever bird" was our parrot, Playback. We sort of inherited him during one of our earlier ATAC cases. Now he was part of the family. He had two cages—that regular-sized one in the den and a huge one in the backyard, where he got to hang out when the weather was nice.

"Wimps!" he squawked at us. For some reason, that's one of his favorite words.

"Can't it wait until tomorrow?" I asked, trying

not to whine. Aunt Trudy really hates it when we whine. "We were working really hard at the, uh, library all day."

She crossed her arms over her chest. Uh-oh. That usually meant trouble.

"I think not," she said tartly. "Even your father has noticed the mess. He was just grumbling to me about how you boys need to take responsibility for your pet."

Gee, thanks, Dad, I thought with a flash of annoyance.

I mean, okay, you couldn't blame Aunt Trudy or Mom for riding us about missing chores or whatever. They're both clueless about ATAC. They really think Frank and I spend most of our time going off on school field trips, study programs, and whatever other crazy cover stories we come up with to explain our travels.

But Dad? He knew exactly where we'd been that day. And he should have known that the last thing we'd feel like doing was cleaning bird poop out of Playback's cages. So why couldn't he cut us some slack?

"We'll get right on it, Aunt Trudy," said Frank.

"Right," I agreed reluctantly as she marched out of the room, looking satisfied. "I call the inside cage."

"No way, bro," Frank retorted. "We'll flip for it."

That's Frank for you. Mr. Fair. Unfortunately for me, he was also Mr. Lucky—that day, at least. He won the toss and picked the inside cage.

"Cool. It's you and me, big guy," he told Playback.

"Wimps!" Playback squawked.

That left me with Playback's backyard palace. Great. It was way larger than the inside one and got cleaned less frequently. That meant I was in for a huge, stinking, fly-encrusted mess.

"Fantastic," I grumbled. "First I almost become a tiger snack, and now this. . . ."

"Have fun," Frank said with a smirk.

Nice. I shot him a glare, then grabbed a bucket and scrub brush from the laundry room and headed outside. Might as well get it over with . . .

The cage door was standing open. Flies buzzed in and out. It was almost winter—you'd think they'd all be frozen or hibernating or whatever flies did when it got cold. But no. They were here, making my miserable job even more miserable.

The cage was taller than I was. I didn't even have to duck as I stepped inside and looked around. It was pretty foul in there.

I wished that cute zookeeper was around to help. And not only because she came with a shovel, a hose, and lots of experience cleaning up after messy animals. Just seeing her might distract me from the grossness.

Oh, well. Maybe thinking about her would help. I tried it as I got started.

Dipping my brush in the water, I stepped over to start scrubbing the main perch. As I did, something whacked me on the head.

"Hey," I muttered, looking up to see what I'd bumped into. A large new mirror bird-toy thing was hanging off the bars of the cage.

Where had that come from? I wondered if Aunt Trudy, who had developed a soft spot for Playback, had started buying him stuff. Then my eyes widened as I realized there were actually two mirrors attached together. And something was stuck into the narrow space in between. I dug in with one finger—and pulled out a shiny silver disk.

"Whoa!" I whispered, shooting a quick look around the backyard. Even as I did it, I knew it was pointless. Whoever had hung that mirror toy was long gone.

I grinned. Then I dropped my scrub brush, tucked the disk into my pocket, and took off for the house.

Getting Prepped

I was scrubbing out Playback's water dish when Joe came running back into the den. Actually, Playback saw him first.

"Danger! Danger!" he squawked. "Wimps! Wimps! Pretty bird!"

I glanced at the parrot in surprise. "Wimps" is pretty much his favorite word. And Joe taught him to yell "Danger!" as a joke. But who in the world had taught him to say "Pretty bird"? Talk about a cliché!

"Dude!" Joe cried breathlessly, not seeming to notice Playback's new vocabulary. "Guess what?"

I sighed. "Okay, let me guess. You suddenly became allergic to bird poop, so I have to clean out both cages by myself?"

"Forget the cages." He sounded excited. "Our next mission's here!"

For a second I remained skeptical. Joe will do almost anything to get out of chores, especially gross ones like cleaning Playback's cages. But he was waving both hands around in his excitement, and I saw a disk in one of them. My eyes widened.

"Really?" I said. "So much for that relaxation break. Come on, let's pop it in."

Almost all our missions come on disks—CDs, DVDs, whatever. We play them on the video game console in my room. As far as Mom, Aunt Trudy, and the rest of the world know, it's an ordinary game console. But in fact it's much more than that.

Soon the disk was in and we were sitting in front of the screen. Our ATAC boss, Q, greeted us in his usual super-serious way. Then the picture switched to a panoramic view of some gorgeous mountains surrounded by heavily wooded foothills.

"Where's that?" Joe murmured. "Think we'll get to ski on this mission? That'd be cool."

"Shh!" I warned him. Our mission disks are rigged to play only once. After that, they revert to ordinary music or movie disks. That means we have only one chance to take in the info we need.

On the screen, the shot was panning over the woods. Soon the camera focused in on a cluster of buildings in a big, grassy, open area. As it pulled in closer, we saw manicured grass and shrubs and neatly tended playing fields. A bunch of buildings, mostly Federal-style brick, were clustered around a tree-lined expanse of lawn. At one end stood an imposing-looking four-story building.

"Welcome to the Willis Firth Academy," a voice-over began. *"One of the most exclusive boys' prep schools in New England, a center of intensive learning in an idyllic setting. But lately, life at Firth has been less than idyllic. . . ."*

The voice-over went on to explain that this Firth place had been experiencing a bunch of problems since the beginning of the current semester. At first it was just small stuff—blown fuses, minor vandalism, that sort of thing.

But then the trouble started to escalate.

"There have been injuries to students and staff that cannot be considered accidental," Voice-Over Dude continued. *"The students at Firth have wealthy and influential parents who are no longer willing to ignore the issue. That's where ATAC comes in."*

"A mission at some school for rich dudes?" Joe sounded dubious. "Um, okay . . ."

"Shh!" I said again as the picture of Firth's campus cut out and Q came back on-screen.

"One of you will pose as a new student at the school," Q said. *"That undercover persona should allow you many advantages in our inquiry. However, we are concerned that living a regimented student life might make it difficult to investigate all aspects of this mission. Therefore, the second member of your team will have a different cover story. He will pose as the handler for the school's canine mascot, a German shepherd. You may decide between yourselves which of you would prefer to play which part."*

"Dibs on the dog guy!" Joe blurted out.

But Q wasn't finished. *"However, I should warn you that said mascot also happens to be a highly trained and very sensitive former police dog. Handling him will not be like dealing with an ordinary pet. He is still a working dog at heart and needs to be treated as such."* He paused, staring into the camera. *"Good luck, boys."*

After giving a few more important details—the wheres and the whens and such—Q disappeared and the tape cut out. I sat back and glanced at Joe.

"Wow," I said. "I guess HQ's really starting to trust us. They don't usually let us choose our own roles on missions."

"Yeah. But not enough to trust us at a school

with actual girls." Joe shook his head. "If we had to have a mission at some fancy-schmancy school, why couldn't it at least involve cute rich girls?"

I grinned. Joe lives for girls, rich or otherwise. "Think you can handle it?" I joked.

"I'm not sure. I might go into withdrawal." Then he got serious. "But listen. We're not going to, like, flip a coin to decide who gets which under-cover role, right? I really think I should be the dog handler."

"Oh? And why's that?"

You can't blame me for being suspicious. Joe does pretty well in school. But that doesn't mean he likes it. I had a feeling he was seeing this mission as a way to get a break from studying for a while. After all, whichever one of us posed as a student would presumably have to, you know, actually attend classes and stuff.

"Face it. I'll definitely be better as the dog dude," Joe said. "I love dogs!"

"This isn't just a dog," I reminded him. "You heard Q. It's a highly trained police dog."

Joe shrugged. "A *retired* police dog. I'm sure I can handle it."

Part of me wanted to keep arguing, just to mess with him. But Q wanted us to leave for Firth pretty much right away.

"Fine," I said. "I'll probably have an easier time blending in as a prep school student anyway."

"True," Joe agreed, looking relieved. "At last, your nerdiness comes in handy."

I decided to let that one pass. Like I said, we didn't have much time. And there was still one more obstacle blocking us from hitting the road for Firth Academy. A *big* obstacle. Actually, two of them.

"Okay," I said. "So what are we going to tell Mom and Aunt Trudy?"

First Impressions

Wow," Frank said. "This place is really nice."
We were in a rental car on our way up
the long drive leading to Firth Academy.
The long, long drive. Seriously, it was at least six
times as long as the street we lived on back home.

We'd traded in our motorcycles for the car in
a little town called Sugarview. Somehow, cruising
onto campus on a pair of tricked-out bikes didn't
seem like the best way to blend in.

"Check it out." I glanced out the car window at
the patches of white here and there. "Looks like
they've already had snow up here."

Frank nodded. "I hope you packed enough
warm clothes, cuz."

"No worries, cuz," I replied with a grin.

Part of our cover story was that Frank and I were cousins. The idea was that Frank decided to transfer to Firth from some other prep school in another state. And when his parents heard that there was an opening for a dog handler/handyman on campus, they recommended his slacker cousin, Joe. That was me, obviously.

"Hope I don't embarrass you, Cousin Frank," I joked as the car climbed a hill. "You know—being a high school dropout and all."

"If you don't embarrass me in real life, I think I can live with you here." Frank smirked at me. "Seriously, though, this should make our job easier. We won't have to sneak around if we want to talk to each other. It would look weird for a student to spend much time with an employee. But nobody will think twice about cousins hanging out."

"Yeah. Although I have a feeling this isn't going to be one of our tougher assignments." I leaned my elbow on the armrest. "How hard can it be to figure out what's going on in an isolated little place like this? I'm guessing we're looking for a disgruntled student causing trouble or looking for attention or whatever."

"You're probably right," Frank agreed. "But we shouldn't jump to conclusions before we talk to the headmaster. ATAC didn't give us much solid info."

"As usual." I shrugged. "Anyway, we'd better hope things are as simple as they seem. That story Dad came up with to cover for us leaving was a little weak."

Frank grimaced. "I know. What kind of school exchange program would need us to leave immediately, with no prior notice to our families?"

"Duh—a fake one, obviously." I snorted. "Anyway, you heard what Dad told us—we'd better do what we can to wrap up this case pronto."

"Right. Otherwise Mom and Aunt Trudy are going to get antsy and start asking questions."

I grinned. "True again, but who cares? That's Dad's problem, not ours."

Frank shot me a look but didn't respond. That was because we'd just crested the hill and now had a great view of the entire sprawling campus. It looked just as scenic as it had on the video.

We drove down there, aiming for the big grassy rectangle at the center of campus—the Green, we'd learned it was called during some quick Internet research. After parking the car in the visitors' lot, we headed straight for that large old building at the head of the Green. Firth Hall. We'd been told the headmaster would be waiting for us there. He was the only guy on campus who knew who we really were and why we were there.

Soon we were being ushered into a cushy, wood-paneled office with tons of bookshelves. A man rose from behind a huge desk to greet us. He was tall and slim, wearing little round glasses and one of those tweedy jackets with the patches on the elbows.

"Hello," he said, hurrying around to shake our hands. "You must be the agents from ATAC. I'm the headmaster here, Dr. Robert Darity."

We introduced ourselves and sat down. "So, Dr. Darity," Frank said. "What can you tell us about the problems you've been having here?"

Headmaster Darity sank back into his chair and sighed. "Where should I start? I suppose the first incident was the fire."

"Fire?" I echoed.

"Well, almost. A fuse blew out during a big fraternity rush function."

Frank looked puzzled. "Fraternity?" he said. "Like the frats in colleges?"

"Yes, we have several fraternities here—it's not uncommon in the preparatory schools in our league." Darity looked at a framed photo hanging among the bookshelves. It showed a group of students standing in front of a house with big Greek letters on the front. "They're meant to be service organizations, but of course you know how that goes. . . ." He shook his head, then cleared his throat and continued. "In any case, the problem was caught almost immediately, and the fire was nothing but a few sparks, really. It could have been much worse. At the time we all wrote it off as an accident."

I nodded, glancing around the dusty old room. It certainly wouldn't be a stretch to believe the wiring in a place like this might go on the fritz.

"All right," said Frank. "What else?"

"Well, there was some minor vandalism here and there," Darity said. "A little graffiti, a broken window." He shrugged. "Most of those incidents also seemed to center around the fraternity rush, and we assumed some overenthusiastic pledges might be trying to impress the brothers or something of that sort. Then there were a few threats and such. . . ."

"What kind of threats?" I asked.

"Just vague stuff. 'Beware, or you'll be sorry,' that sort of thing. Again, we figured it was just the frat guys goofing around." Darity took a deep breath. "But we couldn't explain away what happened next."

Frank leaned forward. "What was that?"

"First, our swimming coach was injured when he slipped and hit his head."

That didn't sound too ominous to me. "Okay," I said. "Um, did he slip on the wet concrete by the pool or what?"

"Not exactly. He was walking into the soccer coach's office at the time. The office was empty—Coach Sims was planning to leave a note for him. But he wound up unconscious."

"Ouch," Frank said. "I take it you don't think that was another accident?"

Darity shook his head grimly. "Believe me, it was no accident. There was thick grease smeared all over the floor. Fortunately, Coach Sims is going to be okay, but it was a close call."

"Interesting." Frank looked thoughtful. I could almost see him taking mental notes. "Is that all?"

"Unfortunately, no." Darity adjusted his glasses. "The other recent incident involved a student named Ellery Marks. He was attacked last week by the school's mascot."

"Mascot?" said Frank. "You mean the dog Joe is supposed to take care of?"

The headmaster nodded. "But don't worry," he said. "Killer is perfectly safe."

"Hang on." I sat up straight. "The dog's name is *Killer*?"

Darity chuckled. "It's not what you think," he assured us. "He came to us with that name from his previous life as a police dog. They told us it was because he used to utterly destroy his toys as a puppy—wouldn't stop until he'd shredded them into tiny pieces."

Somehow, that didn't make me feel much better. I looked over at Frank, wondering if it was too late to switch roles.

But he wasn't looking back at me. "So this dog bit a student?"

"Not just any student." Darity suddenly looked weary. "Ellery Marks comes from a rather, er, influential family. Even by Firth standards." He smiled ruefully. "Luckily, his father was a Firth man himself and knows all about the school's long tradition with these dogs, so he agreed to give us a chance to fix the situation quietly. Hence the new dog handler."

He nodded toward me. I smiled weakly. Great— no pressure or anything . . .

"What is that tradition, anyway?" Frank asked. "All we heard is that the dog is the mascot of the sports teams here."

"Oh, he's much more than that," Darity replied. "The tradition dates back to the days of the school's founder, who adored German shepherds and kept a series of them during his tenure here. Ever since, a shepherd has lived on campus—normally with the headmaster's family." He shrugged. "As it happens I'm allergic to dogs, so ever since I took over the headmaster's position from Dr. Montgomery a few years ago, the dog has lived with its handler in one of the staff cottages."

"Got it." I was less interested in age-old traditions than in the here and now. And some of what I was hearing was giving me serious tiger flashbacks. "Okay, so I take it this particular dog is kind of psycho?"

"Not at all!" Darity looked horrified by the very suggestion. "In fact, Killer is extremely well trained, intelligent, and dignified—a true professional, really. Until this incident, he'd never bitten in his life except when under orders to do so. He's our greatest ambassador and a very popular fellow during Parents' Weekend and similar events. Believe me, everyone on campus loves Killer."

I winced every time he said the name Killer. But I had to admit, the way he described the beast, it sounded more like a puppy dog than a student-eating monster. Whew.

"So what happened with this Ellery guy?" asked Frank.

"We're still not sure." A worried crease appeared

on Darity's brow. "Both Ellery and a witness, a member of the cafeteria staff who happened to be passing by, claimed that Killer's former handler muttered something to him right before the attack." He shook his head. "Many people assumed that Hunt must have trained him with some secret attack word."

"Oh?" Frank sounded dubious.

Darity smiled ruefully. "Believe me, it's possible," he said. "We're talking about a very talented dog trainer here." His voice took on a sad note. "In any case, Hunt has been let go, and that seemed to satisfy Mr. Marks and everyone else." He turned toward me. "But you'll need to be very careful not to allow another incident involving Killer. Considering the importance of that particular school tradition, the publicity could be very bad. Not to mention what Dr. Montgomery would say . . ."

Yeah. Like I said—no pressure.

SLAM! The door crashed open at that moment, making all three of us jump. I looked over, and my eyes widened. Standing there in the doorway was a girl. And not just any girl. The hottest girl I'd ever seen.

"Destiny!" Darity exclaimed. "I'm in the middle of something here."

The girl ignored him. "I need to talk to you,

Dad!" she yelled, her blue eyes flashing fury. Somehow that made her look even hotter. "Did you hear what the coach did?"

Darity raised both hands in a soothing motion. "Take it easy, sweetheart," he said. "Can we discuss this over dinner? Because—"

She put both hands on her hips. "He banished me from practice!" she declared. "Can you believe that? I mean, the Benevolence Weekend game is coming up in, like, five seconds, and if I can't play—"

"I understand, Destiny. But did you talk to the coach? I'm sure he has his reasons."

"Yeah." She tossed her thick, wavy brown hair over her shoulder. "The reason is, he's a jerk!"

"Now, now," said Darity mildly. "What's the real reason?"

She rolled her eyes. "Stupid English quiz," she muttered.

Darity sighed. "You know there's a grades rule here, Destiny. If that quiz brought your average down, Coach is right to bench you until you bring it up again."

"That's stupid," Destiny snapped. "Anyway, how am I supposed to get up to speed with the team if I can't practice with them? It's not fair!"

I traded a glance with Frank. He looked puzzled.

Meanwhile Destiny was still whining and haranguing her father about her problem. Not usually my favorite behavior in a girl. But somehow it worked on her.

Finally Darity held up both hands again. "Fine. Maybe you're right," he told Destiny. "This really is a bit of a special situation. I'll speak to the coach—and to Mr. Westerley, too. Perhaps he can give you a makeup quiz."

"Whatever." Destiny was still frowning. But she didn't sound as furious. "Just make sure you take care of it soon. Our next practice is this afternoon."

Then, with one last toss of her hair, she rushed out like a tornado moving on to the next trailer park. She barely spared Frank and me a glance on her way out. Kind of a bummer, considering her hotness. But probably just as well. We were supposed to be undercover, and I wasn't sure new students and staff members normally had an audience with the headmaster. At least not at the same time.

As the door slammed behind her, Darity sighed and shook his head. "Sorry about that. As you might have gathered, that's my daughter. She's—er—a bit of a handful. I've been doing my best to raise her on my own since her mother died and, well . . ." He let his voice trail off, looking kind of uncomfortable.

"Does she go to school here?" I asked. "We thought Firth was a boys' school."

"It is. She was attending a coed boarding school nearby until this semester." He still looked uncomfortable. "She had, ah, some academic trouble, and well . . . the upshot is, I received special dispensation from our board of directors to allow her to finish out her senior year here at Firth."

Interesting. The only girl in a sea of boys. Sounded like a dream situation for Destiny. At least that was how *I'd* feel if things were reversed.

Darity seemed eager to change the subject. He was already giving Frank his room assignment, telling him he'd be living somewhere called Chittenden House.

"Our dorms are all named after well-known Vermonters," he explained, handing over a key and a packet of papers. "Speaking of names, I understand you'll be enrolling here under your real name, Frank."

"What about me?" I asked.

Darity consulted a sheet on his desk. "Says here you'll be going by the name Joe Fenton."

I grinned, guessing Dad had had something to do with that particular alias. "Got it."

Frank looked worried. "Are you sure this cousins thing will fly?" he asked the headmaster. "If you think it might raise less suspicion if Joe and I don't know each other . . ."

"Don't worry about that," Darity assured us. "Nobody will think twice about that sort of thing here. For instance, our English teacher, Mr. Westerley, was the one who recommended our current head custodian—he was some sort of childhood babysitter or some such." He leaned forward and rested his tweedy elbows on his desk, gazing at us earnestly. "You must understand, Firth is a very insular little community. Families come here for generations. It's a given that if your father went here, you'll be accepted too. Or to take it a step further, if your father was on the fencing team, you'll fence as well. Or if he was the head of one of the fraternities, you'll probably be the same." He grimaced slightly as he said the last part.

I shot Frank a quick look. Was it my imagination, or did Darity seem kind of down on the frats here?

"So when do I get to meet my new roomie?" I asked the headmaster.

"You mean Killer?" Darity smiled. "He's waiting for you in his kennel at your cottage."

My cottage. Sounded a little quaint. Then again, this whole place was pretty quaint.

Darity gave me some quick directions. Then he handed over a bag of liver snaps.

"Those are Killer's favorites," he said. "He'll do anything for one."

"Cool." I pocketed the treats and stood up. "Ready to go, cuz?"

"Ready." Frank stood too. "Thank you, Dr. Darity. We'll be sure to keep you posted on what we find out."

"Please do. My door is always open."

We hurried outside. We'd handed over the keys to our rental car when we first got to Darity's office, and the secretary had told us someone would deliver our bags to our new rooms. All we had to do now was get ourselves there.

"Okay, so what's the plan?" I asked.

Frank looked thoughtful. "First thing I'd like to do is track down this Ellery Marks. Get his take on what happened with the dog."

"Sounds good. Maybe I'll check out the office where the swim coach fell. Talk to both coaches if I can."

We parted ways. Frank hurried off down the path along one side of the Green, while I turned the other way. The weather was cool but sunny, and plenty of students were hanging out on the lawn.

I decided finding my cottage could wait. I wandered around for a while just getting the lay of the land. Then I got directions to the gym from a passing student. Unfortunately, neither coach was around, and the soccer office was locked.

"Oh, well," I murmured as I came out of the building. Checking my watch, I saw that it was getting close to dinnertime. Oops. Probably past time to walk good old Killer.

There was just one problem. I hadn't paid that much attention when Dr. Darity was giving me directions to my cottage. And now that I'd left the Green, I was even more clueless about how to get there.

I hailed another passing student. This one was a tall, good-looking black dude with a preppy look. Okay, so most of the people at Firth had a preppy look. But this guy was even preppier than most. He could have been in a catalog.

"Excuse me," I said. "Could you point me to the staff cottages?"

The guy gave me a friendly smile. "Sure thing. You new here?"

I nodded. "Just got here. I'm the new dog handler."

"Cool. Welcome to Firth. I'm Spencer Thane." The kid stuck out his hand.

"Joe Fenton," I said as we shook.

Spencer pointed down a twisty path by some snow-covered tennis courts. "The staff cottages are that way," he said. "Just keep going past the cafeteria and you'll see them."

"Thanks."

I took off down the path and eventually reached a little cluster of houses. They were in all different shapes, sizes, and states of repair, from a tiny place with peeling paint that couldn't be much bigger than my bedroom at home to a couple of large, attractive bungalows that looked like luxury vacation rentals.

So which one was mine? A guy in his twenties was hurrying past carrying a weed whacker. It didn't take an ATAC agent to guess he was one of my new neighbors.

"Hey," I called to him. "Can you help me out? I'm the new dog handler, and I heard my digs are around here somewhere."

The guy stopped and stared at me. He didn't crack a smile.

"Find it yourself," he snapped. "I just work here."

I was so surprised by the hostile reaction that

I wasn't sure how to respond. The guy took off before I could recover, disappearing down an alley between two of the smaller cottages.

"Weird," I muttered.

I looked around for someone else to ask. There was nobody in sight. Luckily, though, I noticed something else: a large wire dog kennel built alongside one of the cottages.

"Sweet," I whispered, noting that the cottage was probably the largest and nicest of the bunch.

I went over and took a peek into the kennel, which was huge and spotlessly clean. It was empty.

"Doggy must be inside," I murmured to myself.

Pulling out the key Darity had given me, I hurried around to the front door. The key slid in easily. I pushed the door open and stepped inside.

"RRRROWR!"

A mass of fur and sharp teeth leaped at me. Before I could react, I was pinned to the wall by a hundred pounds of snarling German shepherd.

Puppy Love

Who are you?"

I'd just entered my new dorm room in Chittenden house. A guy was lounging on one of the twin beds. He was big and beefy, with dark hair that looked overdue for a trim.

"Hi." I stepped toward him with my hand out. "Frank Hardy. I'm your new roommate."

"My what?" The guy sat up straight, ignoring my hand. "Yo, they didn't tell me someone was moving in! Now where am I supposed to store my laundry, dude?"

He gestured toward the other bed. It was piled with dirty socks and underwear. Nice.

My bags were stacked neatly out in the hallway. I grabbed them and dragged them in.

The guy regarded me with a look of lazy annoyance. "Seriously, dude," he said. "You're not really moving in here, are you?"

"Seriously, I am," I told him. "So what's your name?"

"Zeke."

Zeke clearly wasn't happy to lose his single room. But that wasn't my problem.

"I'm going to take a look around," I told him. "You know Ellery Marks?"

"Sure, everyone knows him. What d'you want with Marks? You friends with that dude? You rich as him, man?" Zeke peered at me with a glimmer of interest. "If you are, you should demand a single room, right?"

"Does Ellery live in this dorm?" I asked, ignoring the rest.

"Naw, bro. He's over in Arthur." Zeke grabbed a cell phone from among a pile of crumpled food wrappers on the bedside table. "Listen, I'm gonna call Darity's office. This room thing's got to be a mixup."

"You do that. I'll catch you later."

I let myself out of the room and headed down the hall. It would be dinnertime in a little while, and I really wanted to get a jump on this case. Talking to Ellery was step one.

Outside Chittenden House, I stopped to look around. Darity had given me a map of campus along with my class schedule and some other info. I'd taken a look at the map during my walk over to the dorm, and I had a pretty good handle on the layout. But I had no idea which dorm building was which.

A passing student glanced at me curiously. I smiled at him.

"Hey, how do I get to Arthur House?" I asked. "I'm looking for a guy named Ellery Marks."

"Ellery?" the guy said. "Oh, sure. You here visiting him?"

"Not exactly," I said. "I'm new here. I just wanted to meet him and talk to him about something."

I was starting to get the sense that everyone at Firth knew everyone else. That could make our task here easier in some ways. But tougher in others.

The kid pointed me in the right direction. I was halfway to Arthur House when I heard raised voices. One of those voices was female.

Glancing over, I saw Darity's daughter facing off against a tall guy with a big nose. She looked pretty irate. Then again, maybe that was her natural look. I certainly hadn't seen her look any other way so far.

"I can't believe you'd do something like that!" she ranted at the guy. Then she let loose with a torrent of swearing that would make a rapper blush.

"Listen, Destiny," the guy said. "I don't know why you think I'd do something like that, but—"

"Shut up! Just shut up, okay?" She rounded off and slapped him hard across the cheek. Then she stormed off.

"You okay, bro?" I asked, taking a step toward the guy.

He put a hand to his cheek and looked at me. "I'll live," he said, sounding rueful rather than angry. "Just don't tell anyone I got smacked down by a girl, okay?"

I laughed. "Deal," I said. "I'm Frank, by the way. New here."

"Lee Jenkins. Welcome. I'm still kind of new around here myself. Just started at Firth this semester."

I glanced in Destiny's direction. "She seemed pretty angry. You break her heart or something?"

Lee rolled his eyes. "Not hardly. She'd never look twice at a guy like me. Well, not unless she was trying to upset Daddy, that is."

I wasn't sure what that meant. But I wasn't too concerned with this guy's dating life. I was much more interested in what the deal was with Darity's daughter—and whether she might be angry enough to cause trouble for the school. It did seem awfully coincidental that she'd arrived on campus at around the same time as all the trouble had started. . . .

"So what'd you do, then?" I asked, trying to sound casual. "Kick her puppy or something?"

"I didn't do anything." A note of frustration crept into Lee's voice. "She just *thinks* I did. See, we're both on the soccer team, and someone told the coach she flunked her last English quiz. She thinks that someone was me."

"And was it?"

"Nope." Lee shrugged. "I already knew Mr. Westerley was going to give her a chance to make up the grade before he notified the coach."

"So why'd she think you ratted her out?"

Lee sighed and kicked at a stone on the path. "For one thing, she thinks I'm some huge Goody Two-Shoes," he said with a grimace. "Plus, she seems to think I'm out to make her look bad on the team or something."

"Sounds like she's got issues," I said.

"You're telling me!" Lee said. "I heard she got

kicked out of two other schools before she came here."

Interesting. But before I could ask Lee any more questions, an elderly man emerged from the nearest building. He was leaning on a cane and moving slowly. But he looked impeccable in a three-piece suit, complete with a flower in his lapel.

"Good afternoon, young men," he said in a quavery voice. "Fine day, isn't it?"

"Hello, Dr. Montgomery," Lee said politely. "How are you today?"

Dr. Montgomery. Where had I heard that name before? Then I remembered. Dr. Darity had mentioned him. He was the school's former headmaster. I hadn't realized he was still around.

"Just fine, just fine." Montgomery peered at Lee through his spectacles. "And I needn't ask to know that you're doing well, Mr. Jenkins. I hear through the grapevine that you're doing just as well rushing GTT as you are in the classroom and on the soccer field."

Lee shrugged, looking sort of sheepish. "Oh, I don't know about that," he said modestly. "They are a great bunch of guys, though."

Meanwhile Dr. Montgomery had turned to gaze at me. "And who have we here?" he asked.

"This is Frank. He's new," Lee said before I could respond.

"Oh? I hadn't heard there was a new student on campus," Dr. Montgomery said.

"I just transferred in," I said. "Frank Hardy."

Dr. Montgomery offered his hand. "Welcome, young man," he said. "I'm sure you'll find a home away from home at Firth. It's the finest place on earth."

Lee checked his watch. "Sorry to rush off," he said. "But I'm about to be late for soccer practice."

"Ah, go on then, my boy," Dr. Montgomery said. "And don't hesitate to call on me if you need any help settling in, Mr. Hardy."

"Thanks." As they moved off in opposite directions, I checked my own watch. Maybe finding Ellery Marks could wait. I wanted to talk to Joe about Destiny Darity first.

A stout middle-aged woman carrying a bucket of cleaning supplies wandered past. "Excuse me," I called to her. "Can you tell me how to get to the dog handler's cottage?"

She stopped. "You're not the new prince of dog poo, are you?" she asked sarcastically.

"Uh, no," I said. "Is there a problem with the dog handler?"

She shrugged. "Only if you consider cheating a problem."

"Cheating?"

She regarded me uncertainly. "You're new around here."

It was more of a statement than a question. But I nodded anyway.

"So what do you mean, cheating?" I asked. "Who cheated?"

She shrugged. "Not sure who's responsible. All I know is whenever a staff member leaves, their cottage is supposed to go back in the lottery. This time it didn't. Cheating."

Now I was starting to catch on. It sounded as if Joe had landed some primo accommodations, and the rest of the staff wasn't happy about it.

After that the woman finally gave me directions to the staff area. I hurried on my way, hoping this cottage thing wouldn't get in the way of our mission. Leave it to Joe to accidentally make a bunch of enemies on our first day. . . .

"Joe!" I blurted out. I'd just rounded some trees, coming in sight of a large, well-appointed bungalow. The door was standing open. Immediately inside, Joe was pinned to the wall by an enormous German shepherd!

Neither my brother nor the dog was moving at

the moment. But the situation looked tense, to say the least. The shepherd's paws were on Joe's chest, and its bared teeth were inches from his throat.

I strode forward. "DOWN!" I thundered.

The dog obeyed instantly, dropping all four to the floor. It turned toward me as Joe staggered a few steps away.

"Watch out!" he called hoarsely. "That thing's a loose cannon!"

I looked at the shepherd. He was staring back at me, looking alert but not at all loose-cannonish. His tail wagged tentatively.

"Come," I ordered him sternly.

Killer trotted toward me. He stopped a couple of feet in front of me, tilting his head up attentively.

"Sit," I said.

The dog dropped to his haunches. Joe was rubbing his chest where Killer's paws had been.

"Hey," he said. "How'd you do that?"

I reached down and gave Killer a pat. He wagged his tail again.

"At ease, soldier," I said.

I was kind of joking. But Killer seemed to read my intent. He jumped to his feet and sort of danced around in front of me. He looked more like our neighbor's goofy Lab puppy than a fine-tuned law enforcement machine.

Joe was looking annoyed. "Killer, come here!" he ordered.

Killer ignored him. His eyes remained on me.

"I think he likes me." I reached down again to ruffle the fur at the dog's neck. "He seems pretty cool. I bet he knows a ton of commands, being an ex-police dog."

"Okay, but what good does it do if he doesn't obey any of them?" Joe stomped over, positioning himself in front of Killer. "Listen, Killer. Sit!"

The dog looked at him. He stood there for a moment, then finally—slowly—sank down onto his haunches again.

"There you go," I said helpfully. "You two just need to get to know each other a little better."

Joe didn't look amused. "Right," he said. "Like maybe next time he won't attack me when I try to go into my own house."

"He was probably just protecting his territory. Dogs do that, right? He'll be fine now that he knows you belong here."

"Whatever." Joe frowned at the dog, then shrugged. "So what are you doing here? Did you find that Ellery kid?"

"Not yet. But I wanted to talk to you about another theory."

We headed into his cottage, with Killer at our

heels. Well, actually at *my* heels. He really seemed to have taken a shine to me.

The cottage was tidy and spacious. There was a list of doggy duties pinned to a bulletin board near the door.

"Great, I'm already behind," Joe said as he scanned it. "Looks like I'm supposed to take Killer on something called exercise walks at least three times a day. Plus additional potty breaks if needed."

"Grab his leash and let's go," I suggested. "We can talk while we walk."

Soon we were wandering down a quiet path near the edge of the woods. I told Joe what I'd witnessed between Destiny and the other student.

Joe looked dubious when I mentioned my suspicions. "You really think Destiny could be a suspect?" he asked. "She doesn't seem like the type."

"Says who? Just because she's a pretty girl doesn't mean she can't be up to no good."

Just then a squirrel darted across the path in front of us. Killer pricked his ears but didn't react otherwise.

"Good boy," I told him. He wagged his tail.

Joe rolled his eyes. "Is it too late to switch places?" he grumbled.

I let that one pass. "So if you don't think Destiny could be our culprit, who else have you got so far?" I asked.

"Hey, who's that?" Joe said instead of answering.

I followed his gaze. I was just in time to see a pale, skinny man in a bow tie hurry across the path a few dozen yards ahead of us. He didn't seem to see us as he disappeared into the woods.

"Where's he going?" I wondered. "Doesn't look like he's dressed for cross-country skiing. Or even a hike."

"Maybe we should send Killer after him to bring him down."

Joe was joking. But I glanced down at the dog. Killer had pricked his ears toward the man. Otherwise, no reaction.

"Killer's not suspicious," I commented. "Guess that means that guy's okay."

Joe shot me an incredulous look. "Who cares what some mutt thinks? What, is Killer a member of ATAC now?"

"Never mind. Come on, let's go this way."

We turned and wandered down a side trail, heading deeper into the woods. It was pretty wild out there. Like we'd entered a whole new kind of world at the edge of the manicured lawns of Firth's campus.

Still, there was evidence that someone else had been out there lately. Cross-country ski tracks. Lots of them.

"Cool," Joe said. "Maybe I can get in some skiing while we're here." He smirked at me. "Especially since I won't have any homework taking up my spare time."

"With any luck, we'll be out of here before you get the chance."

"We'll see," said Joe. "I—hey, come on, you!"

He tugged at Killer's leash. I saw that the dog had frozen and gone on the alert. He was staring intently down another side trail. It was so narrow I hadn't even noticed it.

"What is it, boy?" I asked.

"This isn't an episode of that old TV show *Lassie*, dude," Joe told me.

I ignored the jibe. "Do you smell fire?"

Joe opened his mouth to answer. But just then Killer took off, dragging him down that side trail.

"Hey!" Joe exclaimed. "Stop!"

I ran after them. I definitely smelled fire by now. And something else, too. A sour sort of smell that I couldn't place at first.

A few seconds later all three of us burst out of the trees. We were in a small clearing. A bonfire roared at the center of it. Half a dozen people—Firth students, by the looks of them—were gathered around a guy lying on the ground near the fire. They were all leaning in. None of them noticed our arrival.

"Hold still," one of the students barked out.

The others shifted slightly. That allowed us a better view of the kid on the ground. Despite the cold, he wasn't wearing a shirt. One of the others pressed something against bare skin, and he moaned in pain.

My eyes widened as that mysterious smell got stronger. Now I recognized it.

Burning flesh!

Dangerously Hazy

Wait!" I hissed as Frank started to lunge forward. I'd just figured out what was happening.

He struggled to break free. "We've got to help him!"

"No way, dude." I yanked him back. "This isn't a crime scene. I'm pretty sure it's some kind of hazing thing."

Just then Killer barked. Oh, well. So much for fading back into the woods before they spotted us.

"Hey!" One of the guys spun around. "Who are you?"

"Don't mind us," I said. "Just out walking the dog."

Killer was pulling against the leash. I took a firmer grip so he wouldn't get away.

"Yo," one of the guys said, stepping forward. "It's Joe, right? We met earlier. I'm Spencer."

I hadn't noticed him there at first. But now I recognized him. Mr. Friendly Preppy. "Sure, I remember. How's it going?"

Frank still looked kind of confused. "Um, what's going on out here?"

Spencer looked sheepish. "It's no big deal," he said. "We're just goofing around. Tell them, Patton."

The kid on the ground sat up. He was a redhead with super-pale skin, so the painful-looking burn mark on his side really stood out. He winced as he glanced down at it.

"Yeah," he said weakly. "I wanted them to do this."

A short, stoop-shouldered guy with weird-looking sideburns was standing off to one side of the group. He let out a snort.

"Uh-huh, Peachy here asked for it," Sideburns said in a voice dripping with disdain. "Unlike some of us, he has no shame."

"Shut up, Ellery." Patton sounded cranky. Not that I blamed him. That burn had to hurt like crazy.

But at the moment I was more interested in

Sideburns. "Ellery?" I blurted out. "Are you Ellery Marks?"

"Yeah." He looked mc up and down. "Who's asking?"

"He's the new dog handler," said Spencer, nodding at Killer. The dog had finally stopped pulling. Now he was sitting on Frank's foot.

"Oh." Ellery seemed unimpressed.

"I, uh, was just wondering . . . ," I began, trying to figure out what to ask without giving myself away.

Ellery didn't let me finish. "Look, if you have questions about the school or whatever, I'm sure someone else on the staff can help you. I'm a little too busy to play tour guide."

I felt my cheeks go red. So that was how it was, huh? Ellery was too good to talk to the help. Classy.

Frank shot me a warning look. "Joe's my cousin," he said.

"And who are you? The new janitor?" Ellery turned to regard him with a bored expression.

"I'm a student here," Frank responded easily. That was probably better than the response I had in mind, which was punching Ellery in his smug face. Or maybe ripping out those stupid sideburns. "I just transferred in."

"Where from?" asked Ellery.

Frank named the prep school he'd been given as part of his cover story. By the nods from several of the guys, I guessed they'd heard of it. "So what exactly are you guys doing out here, anyway?" Frank added. "I mean, not to be nosy or anything . . ."

"It's okay, Frank," Spencer said. "It's really no big deal. Just a little GTT tradition."

"GTT?" I echoed.

"Gamma Theta Theta," one of the other guys spoke up. "The most awesome frat on campus!"

They all did a quick little rah-rah type of yelp. I guessed that was another GTT tradition. The only one who didn't join in was Ellery. He just looked bored.

I had to admit it. The guy was cheesing me off. It was bad enough that Killer had totally dissed me. And now *this* clown? So far this mission wasn't my favorite ever.

Oh, well. At least I didn't have to get up early for class in the morning like Frank. Then again, I wasn't sure what time Killer would be expecting his first walk. With my luck, he was probably an early riser.

Thinking about Killer reminded me of the reason Frank and I had wanted to talk to Ellery.

The bite incident. I looked at Ellery again. Peeking out from his sleeve on one arm was something white. A bandage, unless I missed my guess.

Luckily, there didn't seem much danger of a repeat performance at the moment. Killer was still just sitting there, his furry behind resting gently on Frank's shoe. He wasn't paying any attention to Ellery at all. And it was mutual. Ellery had hardly looked the dog's way since our arrival.

That was weird. Wouldn't most people be nervous around a dog that had attacked them? Still, I could already tell that Ellery was an odd duck and a cool customer. So who knew?

Meanwhile Spencer was introducing the rest of the guys in the group. It turned out that Patton and Ellery were the only two would-be pledges. Spencer and the others were seniors who were already members of the frat.

"You've already missed some of rush, but you should check us out," Spencer told Frank. "I think you might fit in with us."

One of the other seniors nodded. "Just don't get your hopes up too much," he warned. "Everyone at Firth wants to join GTT."

"Some of the guys we cut early in rush have

already signed up to rush again next year," another senior bragged.

"Yeah," Patton grumbled under his breath. "If there even *is* a GTT next year."

"What do you mean?" I asked him.

For a second none of them wanted to answer. But finally they all started talking at once. It was kind of hard to follow. But the upshot? It was rumored that Dr. Darity wanted to shut down all the frats.

"Have you ever heard anything so lame?" One of the seniors made a face.

"It's ridiculous!" another burst out so loudly that Killer jumped to his feet. "The frats are a tradition. If he tries to take us on, the entire student body will revolt!"

"Yeah!" Patton shouted, pumping his fist.

It took all my self-control not to roll my eyes. They were being pretty melodramatic about this.

"So what makes you think Darity wants to shut you down?" asked Frank. "Has he actually said so?"

"Not exactly," Spencer admitted with a shrug. "It's mostly just speculation at this point."

Hearing that, I was ready to move on. Then again, I couldn't help remembering those odd little glances and grimaces in the headmaster's office earlier. Could these guys be onto something? And could it have something to do with our case?

After all, what better way to shut down the campus fraternities than to make it look like they were the ones causing trouble and getting people hurt?

Suspect Profile

Suspect: Dr. Robert Darity

Occupation: Headmaster of Firth Academy (for approx. four years)

Previous occupation: History teacher at Firth Academy

Physical description: Age: 47, 6'0", 180 pounds, brown hair, hazel eyes, glasses

Suspicious Behavior: Rumored not to like the school's frats; a little slow to call in help after various trouble on campus

Suspected Of: Causing the trouble himself

Possible Motive: Trying to shut down the frats

"Here we are." I stopped in front of a modern glass-and-steel building just off the Green. "Let's hope the caf here is better than the one back at Bayport High."

"Shh." Frank took a nervous look around. "Don't talk like that. Undercover, remember?"

"Whatever, Mr. Paranoid." I pushed through the dining hall's front door.

Frank followed. "Guess we shouldn't sit together," he said. "Might look weird."

"Yeah. From what I hear, we working stiffs eat together in our own section of the caf. Wouldn't do to mix with you rich and privileged students, you know. Just ask that Ellery guy."

"More importantly," said Frank, "we can talk to more people if we split up. Catch you later, cuz."

"Ditto."

Frank had already filled me in on what he'd found out from that cleaning lady about the cottages. Yet another unfair thing about this assignment. But all I could do was make nice with the rest of the staff and hope they'd accept me. Otherwise it wasn't going to be easy to find out anything useful.

It didn't take long to grab some food and find my way to the staff seating area. As I got closer,

I recognized the hostile dude I'd encountered earlier. He was sitting at the largest table with a bunch of other people of all ages. There were also several smaller tables scattered around the big one.

Everyone stopped talking and stared as I approached. Great. Nothing makes a guy feel welcome like dead silence.

"Uh, hi," I said, feeling stupid. "I'm Joe. New dog guy."

Most of them just kept staring. But I saw a couple of young women at one of the small tables exchange a glance. They didn't look quite as unfriendly as the rest. There was my opening.

"Hi there, ladies," I said, stepping toward them. "Mind if I join you?"

They traded another look. The younger one, a pretty blonde, shrugged. "Free country."

That was all the invitation I needed. I took a seat.

"Okay, it's feeling kind of chilly around here," I said. "Guess it's that cottage thing, right? Wish they'd warned me—I would've volunteered to take the smallest place they have. Heck, I don't need much more than a broom closet. Though the dog might complain, I guess. He seems to like his space."

That seemed to thaw them both out. The brunette even smiled a little.

"Yeah, it's kind of stupid," she said. "I mean, they would've had to move the kennel and everything if you ended up in a different cottage."

The blonde nodded. "Anyway, it's not just that," she said. "Hunt wasn't exactly the most popular person on campus. Guess that rep might've rubbed off on you, too."

"Why wasn't this Hunt character popular?" I picked up my burger and took a bite. It was practically tasteless, except for being too salty. Guess none of that prep school tuition went toward fine cuisine in the caf.

"Dunno." The brunette took a sip of her iced tea. "Maybe it came from spending so much time out cross-country skiing."

"And the marathon training or whatever," the blonde put in. "I'm surprised that poor dog's legs didn't fall off from all the running they did every day out in the woods."

I chuckled. "You don't have to worry about that with me. I'm as lazy as the day is long."

That wasn't entirely true. But it seemed to do the trick. In another few minutes, I was going to have them eating out of my hand.

The blonde giggled. "I can already tell you're

way cooler and more down-to-earth than Hunt," she assured me. "I'm sure the others will come around soon too."

"Yeah," the brunette added. "Especially since you're not too good to eat with the rest of the staff, like *some* people. . . ."

She was watching a stout middle-aged woman march past our table. The woman was carrying a takeout bag and heading toward the exit.

"Who's that?" I asked in a low voice.

"Mrs. Wilson," the blonde said. "She's Dr. Montgomery's housekeeper."

"Who? Oh wait, Montgomery—isn't he the former headmaster of this place?" I vaguely recalled Frank saying he'd run into the old guy earlier.

Both women nodded. "She's like his right-hand man—been with him forever," said the brunette. "But she doesn't have much use for the rest of us. Thinks she's better than us."

Her friend snorted. "Yeah. Not that she is. I heard that niece of hers down in Sugarview can't stand her. . . ."

I kind of zoned out as they gossiped on about Mrs. Wilson, her family, her lack of friends other than Dr. Montgomery, and, for all I knew, her cat. I wasn't too interested in that sort of thing. Still, I did my best to smile and nod along. Now that I'd won them over, I wanted to make sure I didn't lose them again.

Still, it was tough to keep my mind from drifting. Specifically, back to our mission. Could Dr. Darity really be a suspect? Frank and I had discussed it on our walk back to the cottage to drop off Killer. He'd seemed skeptical but had agreed it was worth looking into further.

But would the headmaster really risk his job and reputation just to put the Firth frats out of business? It seemed kind of crazy.

A sudden flurry of shouts rang out from the student section, interrupting my thoughts. Glancing that way, I was just in time to see a stocky guy with greasy dark hair jump up onto one of the tables. He lifted a fistful of spaghetti above his head.

"Food fight!" he howled.

Shifting Targets

O h, man," Spencer said when the food started flying. "Dr. Darity is going to have a fit."

I was sitting across from him. He'd sort of taken me under his wing after our encounter by the bonfire. Lee, Patton, and Ellery were also at our table.

"Does this happen a lot?" I asked.

Ellery shrugged. "Only when both of Zeke's brain cells fire at the same time and he figures out how to bring that whole *Animal House* shtick of his to the masses," he said in his sardonic way.

"Zeke's a loser," Patton added with a frown.

Great. I already knew my new roommate was a charmer. This just confirmed it.

"It wasn't Zeke this time." Lee glanced across the room toward the center of the growing battle. "Lewis started it."

Patton grimaced. "Just as bad," he muttered. "That just means Darity has a real excuse to blame the frats for this—specifically GTT."

"Who's Lewis?" I asked.

"Lewis McPherson Junior," Spencer told me. "He's a sophomore."

"Yeah." Patton sounded disgruntled. "And probably a shoo-in to get into GTT this year."

"Really?" I was surprised to hear that. "So sophomores can pledge frats here? For some reason I got the impression it was mostly a junior-senior thing."

"They're allowed to rush." Spencer ducked as a roll flew across our table. "But mostly they don't make it in until they're older. Lewis is an exception, though."

Patton nodded. "His family has almost as much money as Richie Rich here." He shot a sidelong look at Ellery.

"True," said Spencer. "Plus, McPherson Senior was in a different chapter of GTT at another school."

I couldn't help noticing that none of them seemed too thrilled by the idea of this Lewis guy joining their frat. Well, actually, Ellery looked as if he couldn't care less one way or the other. He was playing with his sideburns and watching as a couple of guys at the next table dumped mustard and ketchup over somebody's head.

But the rest of them looked bummed. Spencer was biting his lip. Lee was sort of hunched down, pretending to be very focused on his food. And Patton was scowling.

"I take it this Lewis kid isn't Mr. Popular?" I said.

"He's obnoxious and a troublemaker," Patton declared. "I can't believe he wasn't cut the first week of rush."

"Of course you can't, Peachy," Ellery taunted, finally tuning back to the conversation. "He might take your spot in GTT."

"Zip it, Marks." Patton scowled at him, his face going as red as his hair. "I just think he's not GTT material, that's all."

"Look, Lewis is okay." Spencer looked kind of uncomfortable. "He just needs to grow up a little. GTT can help him do that if we give him a chance."

Interesting. Spencer was president of GTT. Based on what he was saying, it sounded as if the frat was resigned to taking Lewis even if most of the members didn't like him.

"Yo, Spencer!" a voice rang out. "Ready for dessert?"

It was Lewis. A second later several scoops of ice cream with fudge sauce came flying toward us.

"Duck!" someone shouted. Patton grabbed Lee's applesauce and winged it at Lewis.

And so the battle was on.

I was in the bathroom on my floor back at the dorm trying to wash off the results of the food fight when Joe walked in. He smirked when he saw the chocolate syrup on my shirt and the mustard in my hair.

"Enjoying student life so far?" he taunted playfully.

"It's a cabaret," I snarled back. "Where's your furry friend? Shouldn't you be taking him on walksies about now?"

"That can wait." Joe leaned back against another sink. "Right now we should talk about the case. After all, you'll be stuck in class all day tomorrow."

He was still smirking about that. What can I say? Joe's easily amused.

"Okay, good," I said, wringing out the hem of my shirt. "Because I might have another suspect to add to the list."

"Who?"

I looked around to make sure we were alone in the bathroom. "Name's Lewis McPherson," I said. "He's the kid who started the food fight."

Joe looked interested. "You mean that wrestler-looking dude with the greasy hair?"

"That's the one."

"So what'd he do to make the list? I mean, tossing a burger at the next table isn't quite on the same page as the other stuff we're talking about."

"It's not that. I heard some interesting stuff about him just now." I filled him in on what the other guys had said. "Sounds like the kid's a real troublemaker. Plus, there's something a little weird about the whole GTT entry thing."

Joe tapped his fingers thoughtfully on the porcelain sink top. "Okay, I feel you," he said. "But what about that Peachy Patton dude? Sounds like he's pretty angry that he could be edged out by Lewis for that spot in GTT."

"True. But for that very reason, it seems unlikely he'd do anything to make the frat look bad."

"Good point." Joe nodded. "Okay, let's look into this McPherson guy. I'll send a note to HQ when I get back to the cottage."

"Cool." I wiped one last smudge of something

sticky off my chin, then turned away from the mirror. "Might not play out, but hey, we've got to start somewhere, right?"

Suspect Profile

Suspect: Lewis McPherson Jr.

Hometown: New Canaan, Connecticut

Physical Description: 5'7", 185 pounds, broad shoulders, greasy dark hair

Occupation: Sophomore at Firth; GTT pledge

Suspicious Behavior: Seems to be known around Firth as a general troublemaker

Suspected Of: Miscellaneous acts of sabotage

Possible Motive: Unknown

As we walked out of the bathroom, Joe checked his watch. "Still some time before lights-out. We might as well use it."

"Good call. I still want to talk with Ellery in private—get his version of the dog attack story."

"That reminds me. I found out a little something . . ."

He filled me in on what he'd learned at dinner. It sounded as if Killer's former handler had been anything but popular around campus.

"Interesting," I said. "Especially given what Darity told us. You know—about people suspecting this Hunt guy might've taught Killer to attack on cue."

"Yeah. Anyway, I'd offer to come with you to talk to Ellery, but he'd probably just order me to shine his shoes or something." Joe rolled his eyes. "So maybe I'll see if I can track down the soccer coach and the swim coach instead. Get their take on that incident. Maybe find out if either of them had problems with this Hunt dude or any of the students or whatever."

"Sounds like a plan."

We parted ways outside the dorm. I headed over to Arthur House but discovered that Ellery had just left.

"You might be able to catch him," said the guy at the security desk in the lobby. "He headed that way."

Sure enough, when I hurried back outside, I soon spotted Ellery strolling along one of the paths. I broke into a jog and caught up with him.

"Hey," I said. "How's it going?"

He gave me a shrewd look, as if sizing me up

to see if I was worth talking to. I must have passed the test, because he held up the camera case he was carrying.

"Going to take some shots at archery club practice. You could tag along if you've got nothing better on tap tonight," he said with one of his couldn't-care-less shrugs. "Some of the guys in the club couldn't hit the air a foot in front of them. It's pretty hilarious."

"Cool." I fell into step beside him. "So if they stink so bad, why are you photographing them? Wouldn't a video camera be a better bet? At least then you might make it onto *America's Goofiest Videos* or something. Win some cash."

He actually cracked a half smile at that. "You're obviously a practical man who knows how to use his head," he said. "But me? I'm more the idealistic artist type."

His comment sounded pretty sarcastic, and for a moment I wasn't sure how to take it. But then he started talking about photography, explaining that he tried to shoot different sports and clubs to practice his skills. His world-weary-cynic facade actually started fading away a little as he spoke. It was clear that he was genuinely passionate about photography—not to mention intelligent and quick-witted.

"My father disapproves of all this, of course." Okay, now the cynic was back full force. Ellery hoisted his camera bag and stared at it for a moment. "He wants me to make a killing in the financial world and then get involved with politics. Just like him."

"And you're not into that?"

He gave me a look. "Do I *seem* like someone who'd be into that? If so, kill me now."

I chuckled. "I hear you. So listen, I've been meaning to ask you about something. My cousin Joe mentioned that dog he's handling bit someone before he got here, and he thought it might've been you. True?"

Okay, not too subtle. But I wasn't sure how far we were from wherever this archery club thing was happening. And I didn't want to miss my chance.

A brief look of surprise flitted across Ellery's face. Then his expression shut down again. "Yeah, that was me. Guess I taste like liver."

"So did you—"

"Here we are!" he interrupted loudly. He gestured ahead. "Looks like practice already started. I'd better get over there or I'll miss all the funny stuff."

He hurried forward. I followed more slowly, trying to figure out if his response was suspicious or not. Was he just embarrassed about the bite? Or was there more to that odd look he'd given me?

The archery practice was taking place on one of the manicured sports fields, which had been cleared of snow. Someone had set up a bunch of round targets at one end, and seven or eight students were aiming their arrows at them.

As Ellery fussed around setting up his tripod and other equipment, I watched the archers. Lee Jenkins was one of them. He drew back his bow and let an arrow fly. *Thunk!* It hit the target just a couple of inches shy of the bull's-eye. Nice.

Lewis McPherson was also there. He was joking around and laughing as he notched an arrow. I was only a fair shot myself, but even I could tell he wasn't holding the bow quite right. Sure enough, when he let the arrow fly, it just sort of plopped down a few yards in front of him.

"Epic fail!" he exclaimed loudly, shouting with laughter. "Dudes, hope you don't need me to defend this place when the bears take over."

A couple of the others chuckled. Lee smiled politely. The rest ignored him.

"That guy's a real comedian," Ellery muttered. "Too bad it's only in his own mind."

"Seriously," I agreed.

Meanwhile Lee had lowered his bow and was

glancing around. "Hey, where's Patton?" he asked. "He said he'd be here tonight for sure."

Ellery smirked. "Wait'll you see Peachy try to shoot," he told me. "Robin Hood he ain't. He even makes Lewis look competent." He paused to think. "Okay, nothing could do that. But he makes him look marginally less *in*competent."

"If he's so bad—Lewis, too—why are they even in this club?" I asked.

Ellery bent over to adjust a lens. "Lewis does it because it's the easiest way to get around the PE requirement. He's lazy as a sack of rocks." He shrugged. "As for Peachy, you got me. He probably just wants to suck up to Lee the Wonder Boy and the GTT seniors."

I was about to ask him why he'd called Lee a wonder boy when there was a shout from somewhere behind us. Turning, I saw Patton rushing up. His pale face looked even paler than usual beneath his red hair as he skidded to a stop in the middle of the archery group.

"Guys, listen up!" he called out breathlessly, sounding self-important. "You'll never believe what just happened. This is terrible!"

I raised my eyebrows. But most of the others, Ellery included, didn't react much. I couldn't help wondering if that meant Patton was frequently breathless and self-important—like the boy who cried wolf. Somehow, it wasn't too much of a stretch to imagine.

"What is it, Peachy?" one of the others finally asked, sounding bored. "You lose your room key again?"

"I'm serious, you guys," Patton insisted. "You need to hear this. Spencer just got a death threat!"

Making Tracks

I was awakened out of a sound sleep by something cold and wet on my face. As I lay there sleepily, I smiled. Okay, so dog slobber isn't usually my favorite wake-up call. But if it meant Killer was finally warming up to me a little, I'd take it.

"Good boy," I mumbled with my eyes still closed.

Then I heard movement from somewhere across the room. Hmm. If Killer was licking my face, what or who was that?

I finally cracked open one eye, then the other. That's when I realized it wasn't Killer licking me. There was a slimy, slobbery chunk of fabric draped across my face.

"Ew," I said, sitting up and grabbing the wet mess.

It took me a moment to ID it. That's because it had been chewed and then slimed almost beyond recognition. But I was pretty sure I knew what it was. A sock. Specifically, *my* sock.

"Gee, thanks," I said to Killer, who was sitting over near the door, watching me with his usual look of faint disdain. "Who needs *two* socks anyway?"

I swung my legs off the bed, stood, and stretched. It was early. Just as I'd figured, I wouldn't be able to sleep in with Killer around.

"Okay, fine," I grumbled, shoving my feet into my sneakers. Minus socks. I had some clean ones in my bag, but I didn't feel like digging them out right now. "Let's get this over with."

I headed for the main room, grabbing Killer's leash on the way. He padded along behind me. As soon as we neared the front door, he suddenly perked up. It was as if someone had flipped a switch and he went from Mr. Aloof to Happy Happy Bouncy Walksies Doggie. Seriously. From grim to joyful in a split second.

"Okay, then," I said in surprise. "Guess you're excited about your walk, huh?"

I should have guessed again. As soon as I swung open the door, I saw the reason for Killer's change of mood. Frank was just coming up the front walk.

"You're up," he said, sounding a little surprised. "I thought I'd have to wake you."

"Don't worry. Your best friend already took care of that." I waved a hand at Killer, who was bounding past me to greet Frank with wagging tail and flopping tongue. I could feel a cold breeze on my bare ankles. It had flurried overnight, and the air was crisp. "And my sock, too."

"Sock?"

"Never mind." I barged into Frank and Killer's happy reunion just long enough to clip on the dog's leash. "By the way, shouldn't you be in class?"

"I have a few minutes. I wanted to tell you about something. You know that guy Spencer we met yesterday?"

"Head of GTT, basic BMOC?" I yawned, wondering if there was any coffee in the cottage. "What about him?"

"He received a death threat last night."

That woke me up. "A death threat? For real?"

Killer was pulling at his leash. Frank and I started walking as we talked, once again sticking to the deserted path at the edge of the woods.

Frank started out by telling me about Patton's dramatic arrival at archery practice the night before.

"Apparently the threat came via e-mail. Unknown host," he added before I could ask.

I nodded. "What'd it say?"

"Well, I never actually saw it myself," Frank said with a sigh. "By the time I tracked down Spencer, he'd already forwarded it to Darity. But I managed to convince him I could help—told him I had an uncle in the FBI."

"Improvisation." I smiled and lifted my hand. "Nicely played, bro."

He high-fived me. "Thanks. Anyway, he told me it said something like 'Are you sure you are making the right decisions? Think carefully, Mr. President. It could mean the diff between life and death.'"

"Making the right decisions, huh?" I mused, tugging on the leash to keep Killer from wandering off into a pile of snow. "What do you think that means?"

"Not sure. I'm not even sure it's really a death threat." Frank shook his head. "It seems pretty vague. Just like the rest of the threats."

I nodded. Darity had supplied us with a printout of the earlier messages he'd mentioned. They were all equally ambiguous.

We discussed the e-mails for another minute or two. Then Frank had to leave for his first class. I finished Killer's walk, then returned to my cottage.

"Okay, boy," I told the dog as we turned up the walk. "Time to drop you off for a nice nap in your kennel, okay? I have some snooping around to do."

I'd left the front door unlocked, so I headed in that way. One of the side doors of the house led into the kennel. I planned to kick Killer out there, grab some coffee if I could find some, and then head out.

But as soon as I entered, I knew something wasn't right. Killer knew it too. His head went up and his nose started twitching.

"What is it, boy?" I murmured.

Then I saw what I'd unconsciously registered at first glance. The container of liver snaps that had been sitting on an end table when I'd left was now on the floor, half its contents spilled.

At that moment Killer suddenly lunged away, yanking the leash out of my grip. "Hey!" I cried.

I expected him to dart forward and go for those spilled liver snaps. To my surprise, however, he turned the other way—and dashed out through the still ajar front door!

"Killer, no!" I shouted. "Stop! I mean, down—come—oh, man . . ."

I took off after him, my heart in my throat. What if he bit someone else out there? That would be a disaster—for that person, for Killer, for the school as a whole. Not to mention the end of my own undercover gig.

As I chased Killer across the cottage's small front yard and down a path, I learned a very important lesson. Dogs are fast. At least this particular dog was. Within seconds, he'd outpaced me and was out of sight.

I jogged on, stopping at the last spot I'd caught a glimpse of him. Glancing down, I saw several large paw prints in a clump of snow at the side of the path.

"This is just swell," I grumbled under my breath, casting my eyes forward for more prints. "A dog is supposed to track people, not the other way around."

Thanks to those flurries the night before, there was just enough snow on the ground to make the tracks fairly easy to follow. They led me to the edge of the woods.

That's when I spotted Killer again. He was sniffing around near the tree line. He dipped his head, and I was pretty sure I saw him eat something.

"Okay, boy," I called out in what I hoped

was a soothing voice. "Easy now. Just stay right there...."

I was within a few feet of his dragging leash when he bolted again. His ears were pricked toward something ahead of him.

"Aw, man!" I exclaimed. The snow was deeper here. I could feel it on my bare feet as it seeped into my shoes. "Do we really have to do this?"

I tried to comfort myself with the fact that we were less likely to run into potential bite victims out here in the woods. Or witnesses to my incompetence, either.

"Killer, wait! Heel! Come! Halt!" I tried every doggie command word I could think of. Plus a few more colorful phrases brought on by the current situation. For all Killer cared, I might as well have been speaking Swahili. Or maybe Cat. He let out several sharp barks, bounding forward through the snowy underbrush.

For a second I lost sight of him again. I plowed forward, hoping I was still going the right way. There was another bark, and I adjusted my path.

A few more steps and some scratches from a thornbush later, I found myself at the edge of a clearing. Killer was there too—and he wasn't alone.

There was a woman in the clearing. Her back was to me, so I couldn't see her face. But she was tall and athletic-looking. There were cross-country skis on her feet.

As I watched in horror, Killer crossed the clearing in two big jumps. With another loud bark, he leaped straight at the woman.

"Killer, no!" I howled.

Bad Sports

Yo." Ellery slid into the seat beside me in the dusty old classroom on the second floor of Firth Hall. "You in this class?"

"I thought I was in the right place." I checked my class schedule. "But aren't you a sophomore? I'm supposed to be in third-year English."

"You're in the right place." Ellery slouched in his chair. "I tested out of freshman English, so I'm a year ahead."

At that moment Patton hurried into the room. He was a junior, just like I was supposed to be. Good. At least I wasn't lost on my first day.

I checked the teacher's name on my schedule sheet. "So how's Mr. Westerley? Is he good?"

Ellery shrugged. "You'll find out for yourself in a sec." He nodded toward a man coming through the door behind Patton.

To my surprise, I recognized him. It was the pale, skinny guy in the bow tie, the man Joe and I had seen heading into the woods the day before while we were walking Killer. Now that I got a better look at him, my earlier impression was confirmed. Westerley didn't look like the outdoorsy type. More like a guy who rarely left the library.

"Greetings, people," the teacher said as he dropped his leather satchel on the desk at the front of the room. "Everybody please welcome a new student, Frank Hardy."

"Welcome, Frank Hardy," Ellery singsonged, shooting me a smirk.

Several students laughed, while others called out hellos.

"Okay, let's get to work." Westerley shuffled through some papers on his desk. "I know I promised you a lesson on American transcendentalism today, but I'm afraid I forgot my notes. So let's do some silent reading, all right? Pull out your copies of *Walden*. I'll be back shortly."

He hurried out of the room. "Westerley's getting flakier than ever lately," Ellery commented.

Patton had just slid into a seat across the aisle.

"Yeah," he said, flipping open his copy of *Walden*. "That's the second time this week he forgot his notes."

I wasn't too surprised. Westerley definitely seemed like the absentminded professor type.

Suddenly I recalled where I'd heard his name before. He was the teacher whose quiz Destiny had flunked.

"So Destiny Darity's not in this class, huh?" I commented to Ellery.

He shot me a look. "Why? You got the hots for the headmaster's darling daughter? If so, better cool your jets. That girl's trouble."

"Trouble?" Once again, Patton leaned over from across the way. "You talking about the stuff going on on campus lately?"

"As a matter of fact, Peachy, we weren't." Ellery's voice dripped with scorn. "Guess those big ears of yours only *look* like satellite dishes, huh?"

Patton scowled at him. "I heard him mention Darity, and then you said something about trouble. . . ." He shrugged, looking sulky. "Anyway, I just think you should be a little more worried about what's been happening, that's all. What if Darity really does shut down the frats?"

"What if he does?" Ellery sounded less than devastated. "More than likely, the world will keep turning."

"It figures," Patton muttered. "Just when I was finally about to get into GTT, all this happens."

"Don't be so sure you're a shoo-in for GTT, Peachy," Ellery taunted. "Especially now that Lee Jenkins is turning into Mr. School Soccer Hero."

Patton's expression went dark. "I can't believe they'd let someone like him into GTT," he said.

I had the impression he was talking more to himself than to me or Ellery. But before I could ask him to explain, a guy I didn't know hurried over.

"Hey," he said, shooting a cautious look at the classroom door. "While Westerley's out, I just wanted to remind you guys. There's another event tomorrow night." He glanced at me uncertainly, then returned his attention to the other two. "You know the one I mean."

"Yeah, I know." Ellery sounded as impressed and interested as usual. In other words, not very.

Patton still looked kind of unhappy. "I'll be there," he told the dude. "I just hope the seniors keep an eye on Lewis. This could be the night he finally goes too far." He blinked, suddenly looking marginally more cheerful. "Then again, maybe that'll convince them he's not a risk worth taking. Not with GTT's reputation at stake."

Ellery let out a snort. "Dream on, Peachy. Lewis

would get an invite even if he started showing up to class naked."

The other guy chortled, then hurried back to his seat. I looked at Ellery.

"So Lewis's family is really that big a deal, huh?" I asked.

"Major." Ellery shrugged. "GTT always goes for the big-money guys, even if they don't care about being members."

Patton shot him a look. "Like you, you mean?" he said sharply. "You don't seem to care if you get in either."

Ellery shrugged again. "Hey, it's always better not to look like you want it too much. Otherwise you come off desperate." He slid his eyes toward Patton. "You know all about desperation, huh, Peachy?"

Before Patton could answer, Mr. Westerley hurried back in, clutching some papers. After that, I was too busy taking notes to think about the mission anymore.

For the rest of the day, I stayed just as busy. Classes at Firth were tough. I was a pretty good student back home—Joe loves to call me "brainiac." But even so, I was relieved that I'd only have to keep up here for a limited time.

But maybe not as limited as I'd expected. This case was turning out to be more complicated than it had seemed at first. So I figured I'd better do my best to fit in, academically as well as socially.

When classes finally ended, I headed over to Joe's cottage. I arrived to find him outside with Killer. The dog greeted me enthusiastically as always, though I couldn't help noticing that Joe kept a death grip on his end of the leash.

"Everything okay?" I asked as I ruffled the thick fur around Killer's neck. "You're hanging on to that leash like it's the rip cord on your parachute."

"Yeah," he said sheepishly. "About that . . ."

He filled me in on Killer's escape that morning. When he got to the part about Killer jumping at the woman skier in the woods, my eyes widened.

"Whoa!" I said, visions of ruined cover stories dancing through my head. "Please tell me he didn't bite her."

"Not hardly." Joe shook his head. "It turns out he wasn't being aggressive at all. He was just jumping up on her to say hello, like he does with you." He gave Killer a sour look. "Let me rephrase that. Like he does with everyone but *me*."

I hid a smile. "Don't take it personally, bro. But who was the woman? Does she work here or something?"

"I don't think so. She's some kind of local who has permission to ski the school's trails."

"That explains those tracks we saw yesterday. Did you get her name?"

"Nope. She wasn't the chatty type." Joe shrugged. "Why? I didn't think it mattered."

"I guess it doesn't. I just thought maybe we could find her and ask if she's seen anything suspicious out there."

Joe looked dubious. "I can keep an eye out for her," he said. "She did seem to know Killer, so I guess she must ski around here a lot."

"Okay." I stroked Killer's ears. "Just be a little more careful, okay? If Killer gets loose again . . ."

"I know, I know." He frowned. "I learned my lesson, okay, big bro?"

"Shh." I looked around to make sure we were alone. "Cousins, remember?"

"Whatever." Joe turned and headed into the house. "So did you find out anything today?"

I followed him and Killer inside. "Not much," I said. "Although it sounds like there might be another hazing thing tomorrow night."

"Where?"

"Not sure. I was hoping to find out at lunch, but one of my new teachers wanted me to stay behind for some extra review work."

Joe smirked. "Bummer."

I chose to ignore that. "Anyway, I did get to talk with Ellery and Patton a little." I told him what they'd said.

He nodded with interest. "Sounds like Patton is really worried about getting edged out of a spot in GTT."

"Sounds like he might have reason to be," I countered. "And not just by Lewis. I wonder why he's so down on Lee? Seems like a nice guy to me."

Joe flopped onto the sofa. "Just what I said. He thinks he's getting edged out by him."

I thought back to the conversation. "I'm not sure that's the whole story," I mused. "It seemed like there was something else, something he wasn't saying. . . ."

"Well, either way it sounds like maybe ol' Peachy Patton should go on the suspect list after all," Joe pointed out.

"I think you're right," I agreed. "He could be acting out in anger, or to make the other pledges look bad or something, and not even realize he's hurting the frat itself in the process."

"Or maybe he's mad at the frat," Joe suggested, "because they might pick Lee or Lewis over him."

He had a point. "Let's shoot an e-mail to HQ and see what they can find out about this guy."

<u>Suspect Profile</u>

<u>Suspect:</u> Patton "Peachy" Gage

<u>Hometown:</u> Miami, Florida

<u>Physical Description:</u> 5'9", 155 pounds, pale skin, red hair, freckles

<u>Occupation:</u> Junior at Firth; GTT pledge

<u>Suspected Of:</u> Sabotaging GTT's pledging process

<u>Possible Motive:</u> Trying to make other pledges look bad to increase his own chances of an invitation

<u>Suspicious Behavior:</u> Gossiping a lot; talking smack about Dr. Darity, Lee Jenkins, and Lewis McPherson

After we took care of that, we debated what to do next. "Should we try to talk to the coaches again about that greased floor incident?" I asked. "I heard the soccer team is practicing this afternoon, so we should be able to track down the soccer coach at least."

"Sounds good. Let me put Killer in his kennel and we can go."

I put out a hand to stop him. "Wait. Shouldn't you take Killer with you?" I said. "People won't think twice if they see you walking him around. But if you're snooping around on your own, it might attract attention."

Joe nodded reluctantly. "I guess you're right. Come on, Killer, let's go. But you'd better behave yourself, okay?"

Soon we were at the sports complex. We found the soccer coach's office, but the door was shut. "He's in a meeting with a student," a passing team member informed us. "Should be out soon."

But the coach didn't emerge until it was time for practice to start. "Excuse me, boys," he said, bustling past us.

I glanced at the office door, wondering if we could sneak in and take a look around. I was just in time to see Lee Jenkins emerge. He looked shaken.

Joe noticed too. "You okay, man?" he asked.

"Not really." Lee shook his head. "I'm in trouble with Coach. He thinks my grades are dropping. And that's the one thing he won't tolerate."

I nodded, remembering Destiny's problem. "That's a shame," I said. "Maybe if you really buckle down and study—"

"No, you don't get it!" Lee sounded frustrated. "There's nothing wrong with my grades. Actually, I'm pretty much acing all my classes. But Coach says he checked the computer grade site, and I'm listed as flunking two subjects and pulling Cs and Ds in most of the others!"

"Whoa," Joe said. "That's weird."

"I know." Lee sighed and bent down to give Killer a pat. "I finally persuaded Coach to call a couple of my teachers, and that convinced him. But it's pretty freaky."

I had to agree with him there. As he hurried off to join the practice starting outside, Joe, Killer, and I wandered after him.

"Think this has something to do with our case?" I asked.

Joe shrugged. "Maybe. This definitely makes it seem like somebody's out to cause trouble for Lee, unless it's some kind of computer mix-up. Think it could've been Patton?"

I'd been wondering the same thing. Was Patton out to get Lee because he felt he was taking his spot in GTT? But if so, how did the other stuff tie in? The greased floor, the petty vandalism, Spencer's death threat . . .

"It doesn't really make sense," I mused.

Joe wasn't paying attention anymore. "Hey," he

said. "Sounds like something's going on."

I looked up. We were almost to the soccer field, and we could hear the coach's angry voice.

"Well, where is she?" he shouted. "If she's late for practice again . . ."

"Sounds like Destiny's in trouble," I said.

Joe perked up right away. "Oh, right. She's on the soccer team."

As if on cue, Destiny herself wandered into view. "There she is!" one of the players cried.

"You can get the party started, I'm here." Destiny snapped her gum as she slouched onto the field.

The coach glared at her. "No gum on campus, young lady," he said sternly. "Spit it out and go put on your cleats. You're holding us up."

"Aye, aye, captain." Destiny blew a bubble as she slung her bag onto a bench near where we were standing. Her eyes lit up when she saw Killer. "Hi, boy," she crooned, hurrying over to pet him.

He stood patiently for her caresses, though he didn't show much enthusiasm. Destiny didn't notice. She was staring at Joe.

"Hi, cutie," she said. "Haven't I seen you some- where before?"

"Probably." Joe gave her his smoothest smile. "I'm the new dog handler. Joe Fenton."

I sighed. I recognized that look he had on his

face. It's the one he always gets when there's a pretty girl around.

Sure enough, he and Destiny flirted shamelessly for the entire time it took her to change her shoes. It was only when the coach started yelling again that she finally jogged off to join the rest of the team.

"How about that?" Joe had a huge grin pasted on his face. "Finally, a girl with some taste!"

"What, you mean because she likes Killer?" I said, playing dumb.

"Very funny. Don't be jealous just 'cause a cute girl finally realized I'm the hotter, more happening Hardy."

"You're not a Hardy, you're a Fenton, remember? Now come on—let's book."

Joe was staring out at the team. They were doing drills.

"Are you sure?" he said. "Maybe we should stay and keep an eye on things here. Scene of the crime and all."

"We can try to catch the coach again later. Right now, let's see if we can find Patton. I want to talk to him about Lee."

I practically had to drag Joe away from the field. He finally came when I told him we could drop Killer off at the cottage.

But when we got there, we had an unpleasant surprise. The front door was standing wide open, giving us a good view of the interior. The place had been ransacked!

Dirty Business

Once Frank and I got inside, we realized my place wasn't as trashed as it had seemed at first glance. Someone had dug around in my suitcase, which I hadn't really unpacked yet. They'd tossed my clothes all over the place. There was some half-eaten food on the counter near the fridge and a few magazines and stuff scattered around. That was about it. My ATAC-issue laptop appeared untouched, and so were the printouts of the threats and other papers I'd left stuck under it. Whew!

"Check it out." Frank bent over the coffee table. "Someone stuck a piece of chewed gum on here." He shot me a look. "You know who this reminds me of, right? Destiny's always chomping away despite the school rules."

"She's a rebel." I rolled my eyes.

"No, I'm serious," he said. "What if *this* is why she was late to practice?" He waved a hand to indicate the mess. "I'm thinking we'd better put her on the suspect list, like I was saying before."

It figured. A girl finally preferred me to Frank, and he was ready to send her off to jail.

"Are you sure?" I argued. "I mean, you're talking about a piece of gum—hardly solid evidence." But another look shut me up. I sighed. "Fine," I muttered. "Let's e-mail HQ."

Suspect Profile

Suspect: Destiny Darity

Hometown: Firth Academy

Physical Description: 5'7", 125 pounds, long, wavy dark hair, blue eyes

Occupation: The only female student at Firth (senior)

Suspicious Behavior: Got kicked out of two previous schools; frequently acts confrontational; generally rebellious

Suspected Of: Sabotaging Firth

Possible Motives: Acting out for attention; revenge against her father or other students

We left Killer in his kennel and headed back out. It wasn't hard to find Patton. He was at the first place we looked—the GTT frat house.

Specifically, out in the yard doing push-ups. A guy I didn't know was watching over him. Based on the way the guy was shouting orders, I guessed he was a senior.

"Okay, ten more and then you're done," the senior said as we approached.

He counted down the push-ups. Patton was sweating despite the cold and gasping for breath. When he finished, he collapsed on the ground.

"No time to rest, Peachy." The senior nudged him with his toe. "I want every leaf in this yard raked up. Now!"

"Yes, sir." Patton jumped to his feet. He grabbed a rake leaning against the porch and got to work. The senior watched for a moment, then headed inside.

"I'll be back to check on you," he called over his shoulder.

We stepped forward. "Hey, Patton," said Frank. "What's up?"

Patton stopped raking for a moment. "What are *you* doing here?" he asked suspiciously. "You're not really going to try to rush this year, are you?"

"Maybe." Frank shrugged. "I want to find out more about GTT first."

Patton started raking again, attacking the leaves as if they'd killed his family. "There's not much point. It's pretty much hopeless," he said, sounding kind of angry. "There are way too many people in line ahead of you." He paused and frowned. "Not that half of them deserve to pledge here . . ."

"What do you mean?" I asked. "I thought GTT was, like, super exclusive. The best of the best."

"It's supposed to be. But when you have people who don't even seem to want it, like Ellery . . ." He blew out a sigh of frustration. "I wish Spencer would come to his senses and see that! He keeps saying Ellery will be such a huge asset, blah blah— but it's not fair when there are other people who want it so much more!"

Frank and I are trained in all sorts of methods to get people talking even when they don't want to. But we didn't need any of that to crack Patton. He seemed willing to complain to anyone who would listen.

"And of course everyone wishes Lewis would just go away," he grumbled, still raking. "Enough said there."

"What about Lee Jenkins?" Frank put in casually.

"Lee?" said Patton. "Please! His family doesn't

even have any money! How's he going to afford dues and stuff?" He scowled. "Or will Darity get him a work study job to cover *that*, too?"

Interesting. It sounded like Lee was some kind of scholarship student. I hadn't even known they had those here. But it explained his comments to me the first time we'd met.

Patton still wasn't finished. The mention of Dr. Darity's name caused him to veer off into more complaints about how the headmaster supposedly wanted to do away with the fraternities at Firth. I had the feeling he could go on about that all day.

Finally the senior reappeared. "Peachy!" he shouted. "You aren't supposed to be chatting. We need this place to look good before tomorrow night's event! Don't you care about GTT looking good?"

"Yes, sir." Patton sounded nervous. "Of course, sir."

The senior ignored him. He was looking Frank up and down. "You're the new guy, right?"

"That's right," said Frank.

The senior nodded. "Why don't you come check out our pledge event tomorrow night?"

"What?" Patton blurted out. "He's not a pledge!"

"Silence, worm," the senior said. "I know he's

not officially a pledge. But Spencer says good things about him." He smiled at Frank. "The party should get started around ten."

The next night at nine forty-five, Frank and I were at my cottage talking over the latest developments. It was Saturday, which meant Frank had had the entire day to investigate. Aside from Killer duty, so had I.

We'd finally talked to the two coaches. Unfortunately, we hadn't learned anything useful. The swim coach hadn't been able to tell us much more than we already knew, seeing that he'd been out cold. And the soccer coach had seemed worried about the incident but distracted by fiddling with his computer, which seemed to be having some technical difficulties.

After that we'd tried talking with some of our other suspects. But most were off campus for the day, shopping or otherwise entertaining themselves in Sugarview or elsewhere.

"We'd better get over to the GTT house." Frank checked his watch.

I nodded. Since I wasn't invited to the frat function, I was going to have to just lurk around nearby and wait for Frank to give me updates.

"Are you sure I should take Killer?" I glanced at

the dog, who was snoozing at Frank's feet. "It'll be a lot easier to stay out of sight without him tagging along."

"With him along, you won't need to stay out of sight," Frank pointed out. "Nobody will question you if they think you're out walking him."

I had to admit he had a point, though I wasn't thrilled about it. "Fine," I mumbled, reaching for Killer's leash. "Let's go."

The party was in full swing when we got there. Frank headed inside, leaving me and Killer out in the dark, cold night.

"Guess we're in for a long, boring night, fella," I told the dog.

As usual, he barely acknowledged my existence. This time, though, it was because he was watching a pair of students heading up the path toward the frat house.

One of them spotted us. "Hey, check it out, it's Killer!"

"Killer! Dude!" the other cried cheerfully.

Killer wagged his tail as the pair hurried over. Figured. He really did like everyone except me.

"Hey, you should come join the party, Killer," the first guy said. Finally noticing there was someone on the other end of the leash, he grinned. "You too, dude."

"Yeah," his friend added. "Big GTT bash tonight. Come on in. Spencer won't mind—he likes Killer."

"Sure," I said quickly. I had no idea whether Spencer would, indeed, mind or not. But I wasn't going to pass up the chance to join the party instead of hanging around outside all night.

In fact, Spencer did seem fine with our arrival. He gave Killer a pat and invited me to help myself to the refreshments. Nobody else paid much attention to me. Well, except for Frank, who looked surprised. But just about everyone came over to say hi to Killer. That was one popular dog.

The party was fun. Everyone was there—not only frat president Spencer, but also soccer superstar Lee, bored rich boy Ellery, good old Peachy Patton, Food Fight Lewis, and countless others. I kept an eye on our various suspects, though I wasn't really expecting to learn much in this setting. Not that I was complaining. If there had been any girls there, it would've been an awesome evening. As it was, it was still pretty cool.

Some time later Spencer turned off the music and called for attention. "It's almost midnight," he announced. "Time for us to get down to business."

Several of the other seniors started snickering. "What business?" a pledge called out, sounding nervous.

"It's one of GTT's finest, most esteemed traditions," the senior who'd been bossing Peachy around yesterday said with a grin.

"Right," said another senior. "The deal is, the first pledge who returns with the toilet seat from the headmaster's bathroom in Firth Hall is named Head Pledge."

"Head Pledge?" Patton echoed. "What's that mean?"

"It means you get to order the rest of the pledges around for the entire week," Spencer told him.

Patton smiled. "What are we waiting for? Let's go!"

Everyone raced out of the house, whooping and laughing. I grabbed Killer's leash as we were swept along with the excited crowd. Even lazy Lewis was keeping up.

The entire group raced across the Green. I lost track of Frank, though I was sure he was there somewhere.

Firth Hall was dark and quiet at this hour on a Saturday night. It was actually a little spooky. I tightened my grip on Killer's leash. The last thing I wanted was to have him take off. Tracking him down in this huge old warren of corridors wouldn't be fun.

Soon someone was picking the lock on the headmaster's office complex. I hung at the back of the pack, where Frank finally found me.

"No wonder Darity isn't crazy about the frats," he murmured in my ear, shooting a wary look at Lee, who was standing nearby.

I nodded. "I guess he—Hey!" I blurted out.

The door had just swung open. And Killer, who'd been straining forward on the leash, had just yanked it right out of my hand.

"Oh, man," I cried, diving after him.

But he was too quick. He bolted through the office door, straight toward another doorway off to the side of the secretary's desk.

"Check it out!" Lewis shouted with a laugh. "Killer wants the prize!"

I was just relieved that the dog hadn't run in the other direction. "He must be caught up in the excitement," I said to Frank.

But as I stepped forward to grab him, Killer turned around, planting himself in the doorway. When Ellery stepped toward him, the dog let out a low warning growl.

"Hey, Killer!" Patton exclaimed. "What's the deal? Let us in!"

But Killer didn't back down. He just stood there blocking the door with his body, growling if anyone—even Frank—came too close.

Everyone sort of milled around for a minute. "That dog's gone nuts," one of the pledges I didn't know muttered, shooting a look at Ellery's bandaged arm.

"Take it easy, guys." Spencer looked perplexed. "Just give Joe a chance to get him back under control."

"Yeah," Patton grumbled at me. "Aren't you supposed to be in charge of him?"

"I don't know what to tell you, bro." I took a step forward and was rewarded with another growl and some raised hackles. "See? He doesn't want us over there. Maybe he's got his reasons—he is a trained police dog, you know."

Ellery snorted. "What, you think Darity trained him to protect the john? Get real." He pushed past the others and strode forward, ignoring Killer's growls. For a second I thought he was going to make it in.

But Killer had other plans. He body-blocked Ellery, slamming into him and knocking him back. Then he took up his position again in front of the bathroom door.

"Whoa!" Frank looked impressed. "He must

have learned that trick when he was a police dog."

"This is stupid!" Lewis exclaimed loudly. "I'm not going to let some animal stop me from winning. I can't wait to boss you wimps around all week!" He smirked. "Out of my way, mutt."

With that, he jumped forward and stomped on Killer's paw. The dog let out a yelp of pain and surprise. He fell back just long enough for Lewis to slip past and disappear into the bathroom.

"Gotcha!" Patton cried, leaping forward and grabbing Killer's collar. He was rewarded by his arm almost getting pulled out of the socket as Killer turned and lunged toward the open bathroom door after Lewis.

"Hold on to him!" Spencer cried as Patton struggled to maintain his grip on the collar. "If he bites Lewis or something, we—"

KA-BLAM!

The rest of his words were lost in a huge explosion from inside the bathroom.

FRANK

10

Dead Serious

Smoke rolled out of the doorway. "Keep back!" I yelled.

Yanking up the collar of my T-shirt to cover my mouth, I plunged in. Joe was right behind me.

But it was too late. The interior of the restroom was nothing but rubble. All I could see through the haze was a still figure lying there. Very still.

Joe rushed forward and knelt beside Lewis. He started to perform CPR.

"What's going on in there?" Spencer peered in from the doorway.

I grabbed Killer's leash and hurried that way. "Just stay back," I ordered. "And somebody call 911."

Killer seemed to understand what was needed. With his help, I managed to keep everyone out of the room until we all heard the wail of sirens in the distance.

By Sunday morning the entire campus had heard the grim news. Lewis was dead, killed by that blast. The police had come and gone, though we hadn't heard what they'd found yet.

"Dude," Zeke said as Joe and Killer came into my dorm room after breakfast. "You're totally a hero!"

"Thanks," Joe said modestly. "But I—"

"Not you, bro." Zeke gestured at the dog. "I'm talking about Killer!"

It was amazing how fast things spread at Firth. Just about everyone had heard that Killer had saved most of the GTTers and had done his best to save Lewis, too.

Zeke flopped on his bed and started picking his teeth with a fingernail. "Yo, so what happened, anyway?" he asked us. "Think it was a bomb or something?"

"Who knows?" Joe shrugged, playing dumb. "Guess the police will figure it out."

Zeke snorted. "Yeah, right. Those local yokels? Bet Lewis's family will call in the CIA."

Just then my cell phone rang. It was Darity's office. He wanted to see us.

After dropping off Killer at Joe's cottage, we headed over. We arrived just in time to meet a very disapproving-looking Dr. Montgomery hobbling out on his cane. His greeting was as genteel as ever, but it was obvious he was pretty upset.

"Nothing like this has ever happened at Firth before," he said with an extra quaver in his voice. "Certainly not during my tenure as headmaster! It's unspeakable!" His upper lip trembled. But then he seemed to recover. "Still, we must all pull together in this time of tragedy, boys. Firth first!"

Joe and I mumbled something polite. The former headmaster barely seemed to hear us as he hobbled off.

Soon Darity was ushering us past the police barricades into his private office. Aside from an extra layer of dust, the explosion hadn't damaged anything in there. I guess that was the advantage of the huge old building's extra-thick walls.

Then the headmaster filled us in on some of the details. The police investigation had found that there had been a bomb set inside the toilet. No surprise there. The thing had been rigged to go off as soon as someone lifted the lid. Lewis must have been leaning right over it, since he was killed instantly.

"Obviously, this brings the situation to a whole new level." Darity looked exhausted. I wondered if he'd slept at all. "I appreciate what you two have done so far, but I think it's time to bring in reinforcements. Mr. McPherson is already talking about contacting the FBI—"

"What?" Joe blurted out, leaning forward. "No! If you bring them in, you might never find out who did this!"

"He's right," I agreed. "The reasons you called ATAC in the first place still stand. As teenagers ourselves, Joe and I can blend in on campus and investigate in ways an adult never could."

Darity looked dubious for a moment. But finally he sighed and nodded.

"I suppose you're right," he said. "Of course, the local police will need to continue their investigation, but I'll do my best to convince Lewis's father to leave it at that for now. But he's not a patient man—you might not have much time."

The phone rang. Darity shot it a distracted look as his secretary picked up in the outer office. I took that as our cue to get out before he changed his mind.

"We won't let you down, sir." I stood and glanced at Joe. "Let's go."

We huddled outside the building. "Whoever planted that bomb must be familiar with all the GTT rituals and stuff," said Joe. "Who else would know about the toilet thing?"

"Someone could have found out from a member. But you're right. A frat member or pledge seems like our best bet."

"Obviously, Lewis is off the suspect list," Joe said grimly. "So who else have we got?"

I was running possibilities in my head. "Hang on," I said, realizing something. "If Killer hadn't caught the scent of the explosives and stopped them, all the pledges would have been injured or maybe killed by that blast, right?"

"Good point," Joe said. "But where were all our suspects right before the bomb went off? Is it possible someone was hanging back?"

"I remember Ellery was right up front—he tried to get into the bathroom just before Lewis went in."

Joe nodded. "Patton was right there too, and most of the others," he recalled. "But not Lee."

"Lee? Is he a suspect?"

"I don't know." Joe shrugged. "But I'm pretty sure he was near the back of the pack."

Now that he mentioned it, I remembered that too. "He didn't seem quite as enthused as everyone else about the whole stunt, actually," I said. "But why would he do something like this?"

"Who knows? Let's go talk to him and see if we can figure it out."

We found Lee at his work-study job in the main administrative office. Being Sunday, it was pretty quiet in there. But there were still a few people around.

"Lee?" The woman at the front desk smiled fondly when we asked for him. "Yes, he's here. But I hope you're not planning to take him away from us—this place couldn't run for five minutes without him!"

"Talking about me again, Loretta?" Lee himself appeared behind the woman. He was holding some cables and stuff. "I hope it's nothing bad, because I just got your computer fixed."

"You're a doll!" The woman blew him a kiss and hurried off.

"Hi, Lee," Joe said. "We were hoping to talk to you for a sec."

His pleasant expression went sad. "Oh. Is it about last night?"

"Sort of," I began. "We were just—"

"Lee!" Another woman entered from the back. She looked anxious. But when she saw Joe, she did a double take and then smiled. "Hey, Muttley."

"Hey, Janice." Joe gave me a look. "Just a little nickname the girls came up with at lunch the other day."

"Everything okay?" Lee asked the woman.

She blew out a frustrated sigh, then started complaining—something about a paper jam in her computer printer. Lee turned to us.

"Sorry, I'd better take a look," he said. "Be right back."

He hurried off. Janice stayed behind to chat with Joe. For a moment I was annoyed—there was no time for flirting right now.

But I wasn't giving my brother enough credit. Within moments he got a ton of info out of her about Lee. It seemed everyone in the office—mostly women—adored and doted on him. He had a lot of responsibility and had pretty much been their computer whiz ever since Dr. Darity had ordered all the systems upgraded the summer before.

"I swear, if Lee hadn't started working here this semester, the first marking period grades *still* wouldn't be entered into the system!" The woman laughed. "Let alone the weekly grade updates . . ."

Interesting. So Lee had access to the computer grading records? Probably the same site where the soccer coach had spotted Lee's own alleged bad grades last week?

I wondered what that meant, if anything. Could Lee have altered his own grades? But why? No theories sprang to mind, but I filed away the information for future thought.

Finally Lee returned, and Janice hurried back to her printer. "So I guess you heard Lewis didn't make it," Joe said.

"Didn't everyone?" Lee shook his head sadly. "I just can't believe it. All through breakfast this morning I kept waiting for him to walk by and shake some salt in my coffee like he always did."

"It's hard to believe he's gone," I said.

Lee nodded. "When I left my old public school in Boston, I thought I was leaving the violence and stuff behind. This is crazy."

Just then Spencer stuck his head into the office. "There you are, man," he said to Lee. "Just came by to see how you're holding up."

He noticed me and Joe as he entered and gave us a nod. But he stayed mostly focused on Lee.

"I'm okay, I guess," said Lee. "Just kind of sad, you know?"

Spencer nodded somberly. "I think we're all feeling the same. I've been checking in with all the pledges—well, except Ellery. I haven't tracked him down yet. You haven't seen him, have you?"

"No, sorry. I've been here all morning."

Spencer looked concerned. "Well, I'm sure he'll turn up."

The way he was talking reminded me of Patton's earlier complaints about Spencer being Ellery's champion. Was that true?

Speaking of Patton, he raced in at that moment. Once again, his pale face contrasted starkly with his red hair.

"Spencer! There you are!" he blurted out, sounding upset. "I just heard the news and wanted to make sure you knew!"

"What news?" Spencer asked.

"You didn't hear?" Patton looked grim. "GTT just got banished from campus!"

Undercover or Not?

E asy, Patton." Spencer sounded more distracted than upset. "This isn't the time to start more drama."

"Yeah," Lee added. "Have some respect, man."

Patton looked ready to explode. "I'm not making this up!" he yelled.

Just then two other guys came running in. "Did you hear?" one of them cried breathlessly. "Darity just finished a conference call with the board of trustees."

"Yeah," the second newcomer added. "Until further notice, all frat activities are suspended."

"See? Told you." Patton managed to sound both smug and sad at the same time.

Spencer rubbed his head. "Oh, man," he muttered, for once seeming at a loss. "This is bad. This is really bad. . . ."

"No kidding," one of the newcomers said. "It's not just GTT, either, it's all the frats."

"So what does this mean?" I asked. "Do you have to shut down the house and everything?"

"I don't think so," said Patton. "I heard the guys who live in the houses can stay there. But no parties, no meetings, no pledge activities. Nothing."

"I need to talk to Dr. Darity." Spencer rushed out of the office.

Patton and the other two followed. That left Frank and me alone with Lee.

"Wow," Frank said. "Big news, huh?"

"Yeah." Lee sounded bummed out. "Though after what happened last night . . . Well, let's just say I'm not surprised."

Just then a student hurried in with a question about something. Frank and I took that as our cue to leave.

"Find out anything?" I asked Frank.

We'd just come out of lunch. I'd sat with my usual crowd. Most of the gossip was about Lewis's death, but I hadn't learned anything new.

"Yeah." Frank looked around to make sure

nobody was listening. "I found out the GTT actives and pledges are vowing to continue with their rush despite the ban."

"Whoa! Really?"

He nodded. "Spencer's trying to keep it on the down low. But Patton told me."

I let out a whistle. "Now I wish you'd pushed harder to actually join rush," I said. "If the frat's going into hiding . . ."

"We'll just have to do what we can. At least we're getting friendly with some of the guys by now."

I nodded. After leaving Lee, we'd spent most of the morning talking to some of the other pledges who'd witnessed the explosion. A few of them confirmed what we'd suspected about Patton being envious of Lee for stepping ahead of him in line. Others mentioned that Spencer was Ellery's biggest supporter. Almost all of them admitted that nobody had liked Lewis much.

But none of that was news. It was starting to feel like we were at a dead end with the mission.

"It's time for Killer's next walk," I told Frank now.

"I'll tag along," he said. "Maybe the fresh air will help."

We grabbed the dog and set out on our usual route. Frank and I talked over everything we knew, trying to figure out if we'd missed something important. We kept coming back to the incidents leading up to the explosion, trying to see a pattern.

"There was that blown fuse at the frat function. Then the petty vandalism and stuff." Frank ticked the incidents off on his fingers.

"And those threats," I added. "Then the swim coach getting injured in the soccer coach's office."

"Soccer," Frank said thoughtfully. "Could that be a connection? Lee and Destiny are both on the soccer team."

I tugged Killer away from the pile of snow he was nosing. "Maybe," I said. "But Lee was a victim too, remember? The grade thing. Unless you still think he did that to throw suspicion off himself."

"It's possible. But then how does the dog bite fit in?" Frank glanced down at Killer, who was walking along sedately. "There just doesn't seem to be a common thread."

"Except GTT," I pointed out. "If we take Destiny off the suspect list, everything and everyone else is connected somehow to the frat."

"What about the gum we found after your cottage was ransacked?"

I shrugged. "Lots of people chew gum."

"Not at Firth."

He was right. "Well, what if someone's trying to frame Destiny for some reason?"

That sounded kind of weak, even to me. Frank didn't even bother to answer. He was still staring at Killer thoughtfully.

"Come to think of it, it's weird that Killer was in the cottage when you got there," he said. "Didn't Darity say he'd be in the kennel?"

"You think that could be important?"

"Considering how little we have to go on right now, I think we should consider everything important."

He had a point. I thought back over the past few days, searching my memory for anything out of the ordinary.

"There was the day he ran away," I said.

"I thought that was your fault."

"It was," I said. "But that's not what I'm talking about. I just remembered that when I got back to the cottage that day, Killer acted kind of funny. Plus, there were some liver snaps spilled on the floor."

"You think someone was in there?"

"Could have been." I sighed. "But come on—why would anyone bother to mess with me like that? Nobody here even knows who we really are."

"Except Darity." Frank bit his lip. "And he's the

one who's supposedly so eager to shut down the frats."

On the one hand, that made sense. If Darity was behind the trouble, of course he'd want to throw me and Frank off the track. But I couldn't quite believe it.

"He doesn't seem like that kind of guy," I said. "If he really wanted to shut down the Greek system here, seems like he'd just go ahead and do it."

"Except the frats are a big tradition," Frank pointed out. "One that a lot of wealthy and influential alumni might really want to keep up."

By now we were coming within sight of a place known as the Cottage. This Cottage wasn't like my cottage or the others in the staff area. It was a sprawling, luxurious one-story Tudor where old Dr. Montgomery lived. Janice and her friend had told me all about it during one of their frequent lunchtime rants about Mrs. Wilson, who apparently lived in a smaller cottage just behind the Cottage.

Frank was looking at the place too. "Everyone says Dr. Montgomery still keeps track of everything that goes on around Firth," he said. "And I bet he's more anxious than just about anyone to see this cleared up before the school's rep is damaged. Apparently his favorite saying is 'Firth first.'"

"You think we should talk to him about what's been happening?"

"Couldn't hurt. I'm sure if he'd seen something that was obviously suspicious, he would've already told Darity or the cops." Frank shrugged. "But he might have noticed something he didn't even realize was important."

"It's possible," I agreed, hurrying up the walk with Killer at my heels. "Let's see if he's in. But we'd better not tell him why we're asking."

Frank paused with his hand raised to knock. "Why not?"

"Duh." For a smart guy, my brother can be kind of a dolt sometimes. "Undercover, remember?"

Frank knocked sharply. "I know we're not supposed to tell just anyone," he whispered, "but Darity already knows, so what's the harm? Montgomery's more likely to talk if he knows the deal."

I just shook my head warningly. The door had just swung open.

"Yes?" Mrs. Wilson said icily, looking us over.

Killer had been sitting quietly on Frank's foot. But now he rose slowly to his feet, his hackles up and his gaze trained on the housekeeper.

Okay. So at least I wasn't the *only* person at Firth who wasn't the dog's best friend. "We're looking for Dr. Montgomery," I said, making sure I had a firm grip on the leash.

"I'm afraid he's not available at the moment." If Mrs. Wilson noticed the dog's glare, she didn't let on.

"Oh, that's too bad," Frank said in his best good-guy-talking-to-adults voice. "Could you tell us when—"

He cut himself off. That's because the house-keeper had just shut the door in our faces.

"What a charmer. Guess my lunch buddies were right about her," I said.

Frank raised his hand as if to knock again, then lowered it. "Maybe we should see if he's at Firth Hall," he said. "I think he has an office over there."

"I will not lower my voice!" a woman's strident voice rang out.

Frank, Killer, and I had just entered the large, echoing lobby of Firth Hall. It was normally empty and silent. But not now.

Dr. Darity and Dr. Montgomery were both there. So was a well-dressed middle-aged couple. The husband was standing to one side with his hands in his pockets, looking bored. His wife was ranting at the headmasters.

"Please, Mrs. Marks," Dr. Darity said soothingly, putting a hand on her arm. "If we could just go into my office and talk about this . . ."

I shot Frank a look. Mrs. Marks—could these be Ellery's parents?

"I won't rest until I get some answers!" Mrs. Marks exclaimed. "Do you think we took the helicopter all the way up to this godforsaken place for our health? No, it's because we heard what happened and want to make sure our son is safe here! Isn't that right, Milton?"

"Hmm?" Her husband didn't seem to be listening. "Er, of course, dear."

I felt Killer turn to look behind us. Glancing over my shoulder, I was just in time to see Ellery appear in the doorway.

His mother spotted him too. She descended on him, weeping and moaning. Ellery tolerated her attention with his usual air of superiority. Eventually, however, the two headmasters managed to shoo them all in the direction of Darity's office. Mrs. Marks finally let go of Ellery and swept off on Dr. Montgomery's arm, with her husband and Dr. Darity trailing along.

Only Ellery hung back, shooting us a look. "My folks put on quite a show, don't they?" he said sarcastically as the adults disappeared into the office.

"You might as well give it up now that Mother's all worked up about this."

"Huh?" For a second I thought he knew we were there to see Dr. Montgomery, and I wondered how he'd figured it out.

Ellery rolled his eyes. "Don't play dumb with me," he said. "I know why you guys are really here. ATAC isn't nearly as slick as they think they are."

Office Hours

Joe and I stared at each other in shock as Ellery disappeared into the office after the others. "Whoa!" Joe whispered. "So much for being undercover!"

"We'd better contact HQ. They'll probably want us to pull out if people are onto us." I reached for my phone.

Joe put out a hand to stop me. "Chill for a sec," he said. "We don't know that *people* are onto us. Just Ellery. Isn't his dad a pretty powerful political dude?"

"Yeah. Heard he has some ties to the CIA."

Joe glanced at the office door. Loud voices were drifting out of there. He yanked me a little farther down the hall to a quieter spot.

"Then Mr. Marks would definitely know about ATAC," he hissed. "And probably could have found out we're here. Maybe clued his son in too."

"Maybe." I was still worried. Part of what keeps us safe and allows us to do our job is our cover. A *big* part. "But what if he didn't get it from his dad? Rumors spread fast around this school."

"Think about it, bro," Joe urged. "If someone like, say, Patton knew about us, do you really think he could keep it to himself for more than a nanosecond? Or what about that Neanderthal roommate of yours? Would he be able to act normal around you?" He paused. "Well, or whatever passes for normal with him . . ."

He had a point. "All right, I guess we might as well work under the assumption that Ellery's the only one who knows, at least until we find out otherwise. But we'll have to be careful."

"Always," Joe agreed. He pulled Killer away from the pile of rubble he was sniffing. Last night's explosion had blown a hole in the back of the bathroom wall, which adjoined this part of the hallway. The police had cordoned it off along with the rest of the crime scene.

A little farther down the hall, a door opened a crack. A pale, narrow face peered out.

"Hi, Mr. Westerley," I called, guessing that the

English teacher had heard the commotion from the Marks family. "Don't worry, I think most of the yelling's over out here."

He blinked at me. Then he darted out into the hall, slamming the door behind him. "Oh?" he said in his absentminded way.

I glanced at the door. It had his name on it. "Hope your office didn't get damaged by the explosion last night," I said.

"No, no, no damage here." He straightened his bow tie and stared at Killer.

"Did you notice anything strange around here the past couple of days?" I asked, deciding I might as well take advantage of the chance encounter. "You know—people who wouldn't normally be around this part of the building, anything like that?"

"Strange?" Westerley cleared his throat. "Uh, no. That is, I wasn't in my office much over the weekend. But when I was, I didn't see anything out of the ordinary."

His eyes darted around. He seemed kind of nervous. Was he afraid of Killer? Or was something else going on?

Speaking of Killer, Joe appeared to be having some trouble with him. The dog was pulling at his lead, trying to get closer to Westerley's office door.

For a second I went on full alert. What if there was more than one bomb planted in Firth Hall?

But then I took a better look at Killer and relaxed. He wasn't in alert mode. It was more like he acted when he saw me coming. Or when someone offered him a liver treat. He was whining and wagging his tail, his ears pricked.

"Cut it out, dude!" Joe complained as Killer dragged him forward.

The dog ignored him. He jumped up on the door and let out a bark.

"What's wrong with him?" I wondered. "You don't have another dog in there, do you, Mr. Westerley?"

Westerley laughed, though it sounded kind of forced. "Nothing like that," he said. "Oh wait, I know! I found some doggie treats on the ground on my way in and picked them up. He probably smells them—they're just inside. Here, I'll show you."

He pushed past the excited dog and darted back inside, shutting the door behind him. Joe and I exchanged a glance.

"Is he always this jumpy?" asked Joe.

I shrugged. "He's a little eccentric."

Westerley emerged, once again yanking the door shut behind him. "Here we go," he said, holding out a handful of liver snaps.

He held them in front of Killer's face. The dog hesitated, casting another look at the office door. But when the teacher cooed and shoved the treats even closer, Killer finally picked them politely out of the teacher's hand and swallowed them. Then he turned away from the door and sat down.

"Guess that was it," Joe said. "Dr. Darity said he'd do anything for a liver snap."

"Where'd you find those treats, anyway?" I asked.

Westerley waved a hand vaguely down the hall. "You must have dropped them on your way in," he told Joe. "Now if you'll excuse me, I'm late for an appointment."

He locked his office door, then rushed away. Joe frowned.

"Okay, that was weird," he said. "I don't even have any liver snaps on me today. I keep forgetting to bring them along. So I couldn't have dropped them."

"You know what else is weird?" I stared at Killer, who was sitting quietly. "He didn't even act like he wanted those treats."

We were silent for a moment. I wasn't sure what to make of the odd little encounter. Did it mean something? Or was it just a distraction?

"You don't think that guy could've been the

one who broke into my cottage, do you?" Joe said at last.

"Seems pretty unlikely. But you never know." I glanced down the hall to make sure Westerley was out of sight. Then I turned toward his office door. "Think we should take a look inside just in case?"

"Why not? We're here anyway. . . ."

The office door was locked, but its hardware was as antiquated as the rest of the building. It was a simple matter to jimmy it.

We slipped inside and looked around. It was pretty much what I would have expected. Messy. Dusty furniture. Books everywhere. There were a few cushions and papers scattered on the floor, but otherwise nothing at all out of the ordinary.

Killer perked up a little when he got inside. He pulled away from Joe and trotted over to the window. It was wide open, allowing cold air to rush in.

"Grab him before he jumps out," I warned.

Joe hurried over and picked up the leash. "I think this is a waste of time. We're not going to find anything here," he said. "Let's get out before he comes back and catches us."

Hunting for Answers

This pie is awesome," I declared at dinner that night, shoveling a forkful of oversweetened apples into my mouth. "Think I'll go grab seconds."

I got up and hurried off. But my mind wasn't really on pie.

Ellery's parents were having dinner in the caf. They were seated at the headmaster's table where Darity and Montgomery usually ate. Ellery was there too, though he didn't look thrilled about it.

I'd managed to pass by a couple of times already, trying to hear what they were talking about. Frank had done the same. But I hadn't heard much, and dinner would be over soon.

I slowed to a dawdle as I got closer. Spencer was standing beside the table, talking to Ellery's parents.

". . . and Ellery's been a real asset to the GTT family so far," he was saying as I came within earshot. "We're all looking forward to welcoming him officially into the brotherhood once, uh, all this mess is over." He shot a cautious look at Darity.

"Yes, don't fret," Dr. Montgomery spoke up cheerfully. "I'm sure we'll be able to work things out so the fraternities can resume their rightful place on campus shortly. After all, what would Firth be without that particular brand of brotherhood?"

Mrs. Marks smiled. "Indeed. I know Milton cherished his time in Gamma Theta Theta. Isn't that right, darling?"

"Eh?" Mr. Marks finally looked up from his food. "Oh, yes, yes, of course."

Ellery wasn't saying anything. But he looked over and caught me eavesdropping. His sullen expression changed briefly to a smirk.

A short while later I caught up with Frank outside the cafeteria building. I told him what I'd seen and heard.

"Could Ellery be behind the trouble?" Frank mused. "Maybe that's why his parents showed up—if they know he's capable of this sort of thing, they could be playing damage control."

"Anything's possible." I shrugged. "But what's his motive? He doesn't really seem to care that much about GTT one way or the other."

Frank nodded. "Unless he's faking. We'd better keep a closer eye on him. Just in case."

<u>Suspect Profile</u>

<u>Suspect:</u> Ellery Marks

<u>Hometown:</u> New York, New York

<u>Physical Description:</u> 5'6", 150 pounds, brown hair, sideburns, dresses mostly in black

<u>Occupation:</u> Sophomore at Firth; GTT pledge

<u>Suspicious Behavior:</u> Knows about ATAC; doesn't seem to care about getting into GTT

<u>Suspected Of:</u> Acting out against GTT and/or Firth

<u>Possible Motive:</u> Unknown

"Okay," I said. "But don't forget, Ellery's the one who got bitten by Killer. How does that tie in?"

"Maybe it doesn't. Could be a red herring."

"Yeah. On the other hand, maybe not." I bit my lip. "I hate to say it, but Killer seems to have pretty good instincts. Well, for everything except how he feels about me."

Frank grinned. "You just can't let that go, can you, bro?" Then he went serious again. "But you're right. Killer obviously takes his job very seriously, despite being officially retired. He knew that bomb was there, and he knew exactly what to do about it."

"So what if he sensed Ellery was up to no good?" I said. "Would that make him attack?"

"I don't know. But we should look into it. Darity said some cafeteria worker witnessed the bite. . . ."

"I'm on it," I said, guessing where he was going.

I hurried back into the caf. Thanks to my sparkling personality, I was already making friends despite the rough start. It didn't take me long to ask around and get the name I needed.

"Well?" Frank asked when I emerged again.

"The witness was this newish guy named Chip. I guess he's already pretty popular around here—everyone kept talking about how much fun they always have at these impromptu poker nights he hosts at his cottage."

"What are we waiting for? Let's go talk to him."

"We can't." I kicked at a rock on the path. "He's off campus for a couple of days. Long weekend with the family or something. I guess that's why I haven't met him yet."

Frank looked disappointed. "Oh, well. We'll have to catch him when he gets back."

"Yeah. But don't forget, there's still someone else who witnessed that attack."

"You mean Killer?" Frank smiled. "Too bad he can't talk. He'd probably have this whole thing wrapped up by now."

"Very funny. No, I'm talking about the old handler. The one who got fired. Hunt." Spotting a middle-aged member of the cleaning staff, I called over to her. "Hey, Beatrice! I really need to talk to Hunt, Killer's former handler. Can you hook me up?"

"Hunt?" Beatrice wrinkled her nose. "Why would you want to talk to that piece of work if you don't have to?"

I gave her my most charming smile. "I'm an enigma, what can I say?"

"Do you know where we can find this Hunt person?" Frank put in. "Any chance it's somewhere in this area?"

"Probably down at the family homestead," Beatrice said with a disdainful sniff. "Just outside Sugarview. Brother runs it. Just ask for the old Hunter place."

• • •

First thing Monday morning, I headed down to town. Well, second thing. As usual, Killer was first on the agenda.

But after his morning walk, I left him in the kennel and grabbed the rental car. Fifteen minutes later I was in Sugarview. It was a sleepy little place. The streets were pretty much empty, though there were a few old men hanging out on the porch of the local greasy spoon. They were happy to point me toward the Hunter farm.

I soon found myself bouncing up a rutted drive. At the end was a farmhouse that looked as old as the huge trees behind it. Cows grazed in the fields on either side of the drive.

As I stopped the car, a woman came around the side of the house. She was leading a large Rottweiler on a leash.

"Help you?" the woman called gruffly.

I gasped. "You!" I blurted out, recognizing her. It was the woman I'd seen cross-country skiing—the one Killer had greeted like an old friend!

She scowled as she recognized me, too. "What do you want?"

"I'm here to talk to Hunt," I said. "I have a few questions for him. Is he around?"

"He?" For the first time, a ghost of a smile played around her thin lips. "*I'm* Hunt."

Okay, I admit it. That took me by surprise. For some reason I'd assumed Hunt was a guy.

I did my best to recover. "Um, right," I said. "Listen, I need to ask you about the, um, incident. You know, when Killer bit Ellery Marks."

She tossed the Rottie a treat. A liver snap, by the look of it, though the beast swallowed it too quickly to tell for sure.

"Killer never bit anyone at Firth," said Hunt.

"But—"

"Never," she said firmly. "He never bit anyone. Now if that's all, I have things to do."

She turned and strode away. I tried to follow. But one look from the Rottie changed my mind. If Hunt didn't feel like chatting anymore, I might as well give it up.

On the drive back to campus, I called Frank. "Meet me at the cottage," I said. "I have news."

"Now?" Frank sounded reluctant. "But I told Lee I'd give archery club a try, and I was just leaving—"

"Forget archery club, prep boy," I said. "I have a new suspect for our list."

That got his attention. He was waiting for me when I reached the cottage.

"So did you find this Hunt guy?" he asked as I let Killer out of the kennel and into the house.

"Yep. But Hunt's not a guy." I filled him in on the whole encounter.

"Wow," he said when I finished. "So now she's claiming the bite never happened?"

"Uh-huh. And how weird is it that she's lurking around in the woods near campus?"

"Think she's really just skiing? Or that she even has actual permission to be out there?" Frank shook his head, answering his own questions. "I think you're right. We have another suspect."

It didn't take long to e-mail HQ and get a brief dossier on Hunt. There was nothing too suspicious in her background, but that didn't put us off.

"After all, she's got a built-in motive," Frank said, scanning the printout. "Getting revenge on the place that fired her."

Suspect Profile

Suspect: Isabella "Hunt" Hunter

Hometown: Sugarview, Vermont

Physical Description: Age: 25; 5'9", 140 pounds, athletic build, short blond hair

Occupation: Dog trainer; former handler at Firth

Suspicious Behavior: Skulking in woods near campus

Suspected Of: Sabotaging her former place of employment

Possible Motive: Revenge

I was distracted by Killer. He was pacing in front of the door, seeming restless.

"Looks like he needs to go out," I said. "Do me a favor and take him?"

"You do it." Frank was bent over the laptop. "I want to send HQ a couple more questions."

I sighed. "Whatever," I muttered. "Come on, mutt. Just do your business and get it over with, okay?"

I snapped on the leash. It was too risky to leave him loose outside even for a brief potty break. Especially now, when it was getting dark out.

As soon as I opened the door, Killer leaped through it so violently that he almost jerked the leash out of my hand. "Hey!" I yelled, giving the leash an irritated yank.

My eyes widened as Killer spun to face me. He barked and came flying at me, knocking me flat on my back!

Sneak Attack

I heard Joe call out and Killer bark. Looking up from the computer, I was just in time to see Joe hit the floor—and something whiz over him and thud into the opposite wall. An arrow! If Killer hadn't knocked Joe down, it would've hit him right in the chest!

"You okay, bro?" I shouted.

"What the—?" Joe muttered, sitting up. Yeah, he was okay.

Killer had already turned around. He was staring out into the lowering darkness outside.

"Come on, boy." I grabbed his leash and took off. I could hear someone crashing around in the shrubbery along the path—it had to be the same someone who'd just taken a shot at Joe.

Killer heard it too. He strained against the leash as we ran. I'm in pretty good shape, but it wasn't easy to keep up with him.

The dog led me down the path a short way, then veered into the woods. Great. It was even darker in there. Branches and thorns grabbed at me as I ran, trying not to trip over any roots or get the leash wound around the trees.

Meanwhile the sounds ahead were getting fainter. Finally they faded away completely. The attacker had lost us. I stopped, feeling hopeless.

But then I realized it didn't matter how far behind we were. Not when I had Killer's sensitive, highly trained nose on my side.

"Track him, boy," I urged the dog.

Killer seemed to understand. His nose was twitching like crazy. With a bark, he plunged forward again.

We followed the trail deeper into the woods. I had to strain my eyes to see anything in the darkness beneath the trees. But once in a while I spotted footprints in the snow, making me believe we were on the right track.

Then we hit a dead end. Killer skidded to a halt at the edge of a wide, shallow stream.

I groaned. Of course. Whoever we were chasing must have waded in and followed the stream, knowing the water would wash away any trackable scent. It was the oldest trick in the book.

"Oh, man," I muttered as the dog cast around uncertainly on the stream bank. His paw prints mingled with the footprints the escapee had left.

I was tempted to encourage him to track along the bank until he maybe picked up the scent again. But I wasn't sure whether to try upstream or downstream, and it would be dark soon. So I gave up and headed back to check on Joe.

He was fine, if a bit shaken. "Thanks, boy," he said, giving Killer a pat.

As usual, the dog pretty much ignored him. This time, though, Joe didn't seem to mind. At least not too much.

I walked over to look at the arrow still stuck in the wall. "Weird," I said.

"Yeah." Joe smiled ruefully. "Think this is someone's way of letting you know you're supposed to be at archery club right now?"

"I'll admit, it does make me think of archery club." I peered at the arrow. From what I could tell, it looked just like the ones the club used. "Whoever shot at you had dead aim."

Joe shuddered. "Can we use another term, please?"

"I'm just saying. There's only one person I know of who shoots that well." I thought back to the practice I'd watched with Ellery. "Lee Jenkins."

"Lee's a great shot *and* a superstar soccer player?" Joe shook his head. "Doesn't seem fair."

Suspect Profile

Suspect: Lee Jenkins.

Hometown: Boston, Massachusetts

Physical Description: 6' 1", 180 pounds, prominent nose and crooked teeth, but handsome in an off-beat way

Occupation: Junior at Firth; scholarship student who transferred at the beginning of the year; GTT pledge; soccer player

Suspicious behavior: As an expert archer, could be the one who tried to shoot Joe; was well out of range of restroom explosion

Suspected Of: Sabotaging GTT's pledging process

Possible Motives: Unknown; might resent being a poor kid at a school for rich kids

"It's hard to believe Lee could be behind the mischief," I said. "He seems like such a nice guy."

"I know, right? But he *was* hanging at the back of the group the other night when that bomb went off. And you just said he's, like, some awesome shot, so . . ."

"But that's just it." I stared at the arrow. "He'd have to realize he'd be suspect numero uno for something like this. And he's not stupid."

"Maybe it's a frame job," Joe suggested.

That made a lot more sense to me. "Could be. And now that you mention it, I can think of one person who seems to have it in for Lee. And is also a member of the archery club."

"Is he a peach of a guy?" Joe joked.

I nodded. "Patton. This could be his way of knocking out the competition."

The front door was still standing wide open. Killer looked out and barked.

Joe and I both rushed over, wondering if the attacker had returned. But it was just one of Joe's neighbors heading across the lawn toward his own cottage.

"Hi, Phil," Joe called out as the guy waved.

"Hey, that reminds me," I murmured. "We still need to track down that Chip guy who witnessed Ellery getting bitten."

"What a coincidence. Phil there was the one who told me he was away. I think they're pretty good friends." Joe raised his voice. "Yo, Phil. Any idea if Chip's back on campus yet?"

Phil came toward us. I recognized him as part of the grounds crew. "Nope," he said, sounding kind of bummed. "Actually, it's funny you should ask. I just got a text from him saying he's not coming back."

"What?" said Joe. "Why not?"

Phil shrugged. "Got me. Said he'd explain later. But he quit his job and he's out of here for good."

"Hear anything from HQ yet?" Joe asked quietly, pausing beside my table on his way toward the cafeteria line.

I looked around to make sure none of my tablemates had heard him. "Nothing yet," I hissed.

We'd sent a note earlier, hoping ATAC could track down where this Chip guy had gone. But by the time we left for dinner, we hadn't heard back.

As usual, I'd found a seat with the GTT crew. Unfortunately, nobody seemed interested in talking about frat issues for once. I'd even tried to launch the subject a couple of times. No luck.

By the time I met up with Joe after dinner, I was feeling frustrated. "Got anything?" I asked him.

He shrugged. "My peeps spent half the meal gossiping about Chip's sudden departure," he reported. "But I don't think any of them actually knew anything. He wasn't here for long, remember."

I sighed. This mission was going nowhere fast. "We have all these suspects, but none of the scenarios really make sense," I complained. "And the more we find out, the less we seem to know."

"Let's grab the pooch, then see what we can sniff out," Joe said. "Maybe we can find Lee and talk to him—or at least figure out if he has an alibi for the time I almost became a shish kebab."

By the time I fell into bed that night, we still didn't have any solid answers. I lay awake, staring into the darkness and listening to Zeke snore.

There were just too many loose ends going in all directions. Too many suspects. Not enough solid facts.

If Darity wanted to shut down the frats, would he really go so far as to set that bomb? It seemed pretty unlikely.

Hunt Hunter had a better motive. But could she have pulled off all the mischief without being spotted? That seemed unlikely too.

And what about Patton? He too had a decent

motive. But it was hard to believe he could have pulled off some of the stuff. The guy was pretty much an open book, with every thought and emotion playing out on his freckled face. He just didn't have the personality to keep so many secrets.

Then there were our other suspects, most with pretty weak or downright nonexistent motives. Lee. Westerley. Destiny. Ellery.

I finally drifted off to sleep. But the questions haunted me all through my dreams.

BZZZ! BZZZ!

I swam upward out of sleep. My head was filled with confusing images of various suspects buzzing around me like bees.

My eyes flew open to total darkness. It was the middle of the night. And I realized the buzzing noise I heard was my cell phone.

It had to be well after midnight. Who would be calling me now?

Joe, I realized. Maybe he'd had some kind of breakthrough.

The thought woke me up enough to reach over and grapple around on the bedside table. I could hear Zeke mumble something cranky from the other bed. My hand finally closed around the phone.

"H'lo?" I mumbled into it.

All I heard for a second was the sound of screaming. I pressed the phone to my ear, wondering if this was still a dream.

"Hello?" I said again.

"His face!" an unrecognizable voice shrieked into my ear. *"Oh my God—it's eating his face off!"*

Cutting to the Chase

I raced through the darkness, my heart in my throat. Frank's call had yanked me out of a sound sleep.

"I think something terrible has happened at the frat house," he'd said. "I'm already on my way."

"What?" I'd mumbled sleepily, not sure if I was awake or dreaming.

"Someone called. Not sure, but I think it might've been Spencer. Hurry up!"

I'd pulled on some clothes and taken off. Killer had barked as I passed, but I'd left him behind. Whatever was going on, it sounded like it might be too late for him to save the day this time.

Frank and I almost collided outside the GTT

house. All the lights on the first floor were blazing, and people were milling around outside despite the frigid night air.

"What's going on?" Frank shouted as we pushed our way toward the door. "Where's Spencer?"

"Here I am!" Spencer came rushing toward us, his face pinched and anxious. "Thanks for coming, Frank. I—I didn't know who else to call, and since you said someone in your family was with the FBI . . ."

"It's okay. Just tell us what happened," said Frank.

Spencer looked at me as if he was wondering what I was doing there. But he just nodded. "Come inside."

We followed him into the house. Someone was lying on the couch with a wet rag over his face.

"Is that Patton?" I asked, noting the red hair on the figure's arms.

Spencer bit his lip. He looked really upset now. "Don't worry, I already called an ambulance."

Then he told us what had happened. It turned out the frat had been holding a secret late-night pledge ritual in defiance of the ban. This one was another long-running GTT tradition. The pledges were supposed to go blindfolded into a room in the basement. There, they had to eat and drink various unseen substances and smear others onto their skin.

"It can get pretty gross, but it's just some harmless fun," Spencer insisted. "Nobody gets hurt beyond maybe a little barfing. Usually." He shot a look at Patton, who had just started groaning softly from under the rag.

"So what went wrong?" Frank asked.

Spencer sighed and closed his eyes for a second. "Patton volunteered to go first," he said. "For a while everything went fine. He ate and drank everything, and didn't even hurl. We were all pretty proud of him, since he can be kind of a wuss."

That didn't seem very nice, considering. But I kept quiet.

"Then he came to this bowl of raw eggs he was supposed to smear on his face." Spencer swallowed hard. "As soon as he did it, he just started, like, screaming."

Another senior had wandered into the room and heard him. "Yeah," he put in, looking pale. "At first we just thought it was Peachy being Peachy."

"But then we realized he wasn't just being dramatic," Spencer went on. "Someone must have added something to the egg goop. Like acid or something." He shuddered. "It just started burning away his skin!"

I glanced over at Patton again, just in time to see him shift positions. A corner of the rag fell away, revealing one of his cheeks.

Bile rose to my throat. The dude's face looked like raw hamburger meat. It was basically one big oozing blister. Ouch. I have a pretty strong stomach, but I had to turn away.

"I guess I called you in a panic, Frank, thinking you might be able to help get us out of this mess," Spencer admitted. "You know—since we're not supposed to be doing any frat stuff right now. But when I got a closer look at Patton's face, I knew I'd just have to face the music."

The wail of an ambulance cut through the commotion. Patton let out another moan.

"Did anyone call Dr. Darity?" I asked.

Spencer shook his head, then squared his shoulders. "No. But I guess I'll go do that now. It might be better to tell him in person—I'm sure the ambulance has woken him up by now."

He hurried off. A moment later the paramedics bustled in and then out again with Patton.

"Think he's going to be okay?" I asked.

"Hope so." Frank glanced around. "But let's let the experts take care of that part. We should try to figure out what happened."

We stuck around for a while, trying to question

people. But everyone was too upset to make much sense. The guys who'd put together the stuff for the ritual explained that they'd set it up that morning before classes. A few of the things had spent the day in the fridge, and others had been in the basement. Either way, just about anyone could have messed with them. The house was never locked.

The paramedics had taken the acid-laced egg bowl away with them. So that left us pretty much nowhere. We took a quick look around the basement but didn't find anything useful down there.

I noticed Frank stifling a yawn. I knew how he felt.

"Should we head out?" I said. "We're not doing much good here."

"Might as well," said Frank. "Can you e-mail HQ about this? I'd do it, but Zeke—"

"No problem. I'm on it."

We left the house and headed down the path. "Here we are," Frank said as we reached the turn-off for my cottage. "I'll see you in the—"

"WOOF!"

A big, furry shape burst out of the darkness. Killer. He flung himself happily at Frank.

"What the—," I muttered. I took off for the cottage.

Frank followed, with Killer frisking at his heels. "Did you run out so fast you left the door open?" he panted.

"Dude! I was sleepy, but not *that* sleepy!" I put on a burst of speed as we neared the cottage. The door was standing ajar.

We did the ATAC agent thing, slowing down and creeping up on the place. But I guess Killer didn't get the memo to be careful. He just trotted right on in.

"Oh, man!" I said to Frank. "Stay here and back me up. I'm going in."

Leaving my brother lurking just outside, I stepped carefully inside. Standing there in front of the refrigerator was . . . Destiny?!?

"What are you doing here?" I blurted out in surprise.

She turned to face me. She was dressed in sweatpants and an oversized T-shirt, and her thick hair was rumpled. Somehow, it all made her look hotter than ever.

"Hi, cutie. Guess you caught me this time." She didn't even sound embarrassed.

"This time?" I echoed. "Wait—are you the one who broke in here those other times?"

"Guilty. I've been checking you out ever since you got here." She sashayed toward me. The way she was smiling at me was kind of distracting, but I did my best to keep myself on message.

"So that *was* your gum," I murmured, casting a glance over my shoulder in the direction of the still-hidden Frank.

"What was that?"

"Uh, nothing." I wondered how much Destiny had seen while snooping around. Did she suspect why I was really here? "Why have you been spying on me?"

She was standing right in front of me by now. Tilting her head to one side, she looked at me appraisingly.

"Why do you think? You're a guy, right? And in case you haven't noticed, I'm a girl." She sort of stretched when she said that. Gulp. Yeah, definitely distracting.

"In case you haven't noticed, there are better ways to ask a guy out than creeping around raiding his refrigerator," I countered.

She laughed a lot harder than the lame joke warranted. "You're awesome," she said, taking yet another step closer. "It's going to be a blast sneaking around with you. Not to mention watching Dad's head explode when he finds out I've been dating the help."

"Come on," I said, trying not to notice how

good she smelled. "Your dad doesn't seem like the type to mind something like that."

"Don't be so sure." She smirked. "I bet he'd freak if he knew one of his oh-so-proper teachers was sneaking around with that gross dog woman he fired too. . . ."

Despite being totally distracted, my mind immediately picked up on that one. Of course! Mr. Westerley was secretly dating Hunt Hunter!

That cleared up a few things. For one, it explained the incident with Killer outside the teacher's office. Hunt must have been inside, and the dog had smelled her and gotten excited to see his old friend. When Westerley had gone back inside, he'd grabbed some liver snaps from Hunt and told her to climb out that open window.

This explained catching Westerley tiptoeing along those snowy trails, too, and seeing Hunt skiing in the woods. The two of them must have set up a regular meeting spot out there. I guessed this also meant Hunt was probably the one who'd let Killer loose in the cottage right before I arrived—maybe she'd stopped in to visit him on her way to see her boyfriend. And when she saw me coming, she hadn't had time to put him back in the kennel.

"Hey," Destiny purred, breaking me out of my

thoughts. She poked me in the chest with one finger and leaned so close I could smell her gum. Spearmint. "What do you think? Want to have some fun, or are you too afraid of my dad?"

I gulped, not sure what to say to that. Okay, I knew what I *wanted* to say. But I was here for work, not pleasure.

Someone cleared their throat behind me. I glanced back and saw Frank stepping into view in the doorway.

"Excuse me," he said loudly. "I hope I'm not interrupting anything."

Destiny scowled and backed away. "As a matter of fact, you are."

"Sorry," said Frank, not sounding sorry at all. "But I'm afraid I have to borrow my cousin right now."

For a second Destiny looked ready to argue. Or maybe even haul off and slap him one like she'd done to Lee that time.

Instead she whirled and stomped toward the door. "Fine," she tossed over her shoulder. "But I'll be back, Joe. You can count on it. We're meant to be together."

Then she was gone.

"Don't take this the wrong way," Frank said. "But your new girlfriend's kind of a psycho."

"Psycho, maybe. Hot? Definitely."

Just then my laptop let out a beep. It was an e-mail from HQ. Talk about timing!

The researchers had finally tracked down Chip. "Says he's in New York," I said, scanning the message. "Just started a job with Marks Industries."

"Marks Industries?" Frank raised an eyebrow. "As in Ellery Marks?" His phone rang. He pulled it out of his pocket, looking surprised. "Hello?" he said into it.

He listened for a moment, looking increasingly worried. Finally he spoke again.

"Got it," he told the caller. "We'll be right there."

"Who was that?"

"Spencer. He just got out of his meeting with Darity." Frank grabbed Killer's leash off its hook and attached it to the dog's collar. "When he got back to the house, he found out nobody's seen Ellery since the beginning of the ritual. Considering what happened to Patton, everyone's pretty worried."

"No wonder," I said, catching on right away. "Whoever's doing this seems to be targeting the pledges. We'd better track Ellery down and make sure he's safe."

We grabbed a couple of flashlights and hurried back out into the night. This time Killer came along. I figured he might come in handy.

When we reached the frat house, everyone was still there—and more anxious than ever. "We've been trying Ellery's phone," one of the seniors said. "No answer."

"That's not like him," someone else added. "He always answers his phone. Even during class. The teachers hate it."

Just then Dr. Darity arrived on the scene. He looked rumpled and sleepy and a little confused. But he did his best to take charge, ordering everyone back to their dorms.

But no one paid much attention. I guessed they were all too worried. Especially Spencer, who looked really freaked out.

"I'll never forgive myself if another pledge is hurt—especially Ellery," he moaned. "We have to find him!"

"Leave that to me," Darity put in. "I imagine Ellery just went to visit his parents or something."

Yeah, right. Ellery just had a sudden urge to spend time with Mommy and Daddy? In the middle of the night? During a frat ritual?

"We need to know he's okay, Dr. D!" someone called out.

Another pledge nodded. "Yeah. Ellery's our brother."

I stepped toward the headmaster. "The more

people we have looking, the more likely we are to find him," I said. "You might as well let them help."

Darity looked ready to argue. But then he sighed. "Fine," he said. "I suppose we'll all feel better once we locate him."

He sent a pledge off to the guest housing to see if Ellery was with his parents. In the meantime, Lee noticed Killer sitting by Frank's side.

"Hey, he's a police dog, right?" he said. "Let's give him something of Ellery's to smell. Maybe he can track him."

Soon someone was shoving a jacket in front of Killer's nose. The dog sniffed at it, then glanced at Frank.

"Find him, boy," Frank urged. Then he leaned down and unclipped his leash.

That was all Killer was waiting for. He took off through the door, barking loudly.

"Are you sure that was a good idea?" I asked Frank as we both sprinted after him, with Darity and most of GTT right behind us. "How do we know he's really tracking and not just making a break for freedom?"

"Look." Frank pointed. Killer had stopped at the path. His nose was to the ground, sniffing around busily.

It was actually pretty impressive. The dog would follow one trail for a yard or two, then double back and try another.

Finally he seemed to find the scent he wanted. With a flurry of barks, he took off again.

For the next half hour, Killer led us all on a merry chase. We ran across campus, then headed into the woods. Then deeper into the woods. Really deep.

There was a moon, and Frank and I had our flashlights. Even so, it wasn't easy going. The footing stunk. There were vines and thorns everywhere.

I spent most of my spare energy trying to keep Killer in sight. But once in a while I glanced back to see how the others were keeping up. The group kept shrinking with every passing minute.

When Killer paused at the bank of a creek, Frank looked worried. "Uh-oh," he said. "Hope he doesn't lose the trail here."

But Killer leaped across the creek. He only sniffed around for a second before he let out an excited bark. Then he continued to follow his nose.

Farther, deeper into the woods . . . Once again, I couldn't help wondering if the dog was just messing with us. For all we knew, he could be tracking a deer or a squirrel. That police training had been a long time ago.

"Look!" Frank shouted, pointing ahead.

I gasped as I saw what he'd just seen. Lights! Something was definitely flickering through the trees.

"What's that?" Dr. Darity was breathing so hard he could barely get the words out as he caught up to us.

I was surprised. And kind of impressed. By now almost everyone had dropped back except for Spencer and two or three others. I hadn't even noticed that the headmaster was among them.

"Looks like someone's up there," said Frank.

"But who?" Darity sounded confused. "This part of the forest is completely uninhabited. It's all Firth land in this direction."

"Well, somebody's up there," I said, my gaze trained on the flickering light. "Come on, let's find out who."

Killer had disappeared by now. From somewhere up ahead, he let out several loud, fierce barks.

"Hurry!" Frank took off, with the rest of us right behind him.

We burst out into a clearing. A small but tidy hunting hut stood in the middle. That was where the light was coming from. It spilled out through the windows into the clearing, illuminating a startling sight.

Ellery was standing there. He was holding a huge knife in one hand. And he was staring angrily at his own father!

Blood Brothers

I froze, not sure what to do. Nobody else seemed to know how to react either.

Except Killer. He lunged forward, knocking Ellery down. The knife flew out of his hand.

I dove for it. My hand closed over the handle, and I breathed a sigh of relief.

"Hey!" Ellery yelled.

Then everyone started talking at once. Dr. Darity tried to call for quiet, but nobody paid any attention.

"Silence!" Mr. Marks thundered.

That did the trick. When that guy talked, people listened. It was no wonder he was a huge business success.

"That's better," he grumbled. "I'm not sure what you're all doing here, but this is no business of yours. I'll thank you to leave my son and me alone. Now."

I opened my mouth to protest. But Ellery spoke first.

"Get real, Dad," he said. For once he didn't look calm, cool, collected, and cynical. There was a haunted look in his eyes. "It's too late. They're all going to know now."

"Know what?" Spencer sounded confused. I knew how he felt.

Ellery swallowed hard. "It was me," he said. "It was all me. All the graffiti, the threats—I did it because I don't want to be in GTT." He glared at his father. "And I especially didn't want to join the Brothers of Erebus."

"The whos of what?" Joe asked.

Mr. Marks looked furious. "Shut up!" he hissed at his son.

But Ellery wouldn't be stopped. "It's this stupid secret society," he told us all. "Like a frat within a frat—the members are all from GTT, but not all the GTT brothers even know it exists. It's like the power center of GTT. Of Firth, for that matter."

"That's enough." The tone of Mr. Marks's voice made my blood run cold.

"Dr. Montgomery is a member," Ellery went on. "And my dear old pop here was president in his day." He turned and sneered at Spencer. "And don't look so shocked, Mr. President. I knew all along that's why you were such a big supporter of my bid. You knew my father's rep, and you wanted to make sure you were the one who brought in the next generation."

"You mean you're in this Erebus group too?" Joe asked Spencer.

Spencer didn't respond. Or meet his eye. That seemed answer enough.

Ellery shrugged. "I always knew I wasn't cut out for that kind of thing. I don't crave power or any of that. I just want to play with my cameras." He shot his father another sour look. "But that was never enough, was it, Dad?"

"But why'd you cause all that trouble?" Joe asked. "Why not just say you didn't want to pledge?"

"I tried. Nobody believed me. After all," he added, his old sarcastic tone back full force, "*everybody* wants to be in GTT." He shook his head. "I did everything I could to make myself undesirable as a brother. But nothing worked. Not talking back to the actives, or refusing to take part in the hazing, or making fun of the whole rush thing. If anything, it seemed to make them want me more."

"Ellery . . . ," Spencer began in a choked-up voice.

"And then I saw that you guys were planning to admit Lewis despite his even worse personality issues." Ellery shook his head. "So I decided to stop messing around with the minor-league stuff. Desperate times called for desperate measures."

"Like attacking your own father?" I asked, glancing at the knife in my hand.

"That's pretty desperate," Joe said.

"That's not what was happening here," Mr. Marks said. His voice suddenly sounded less commanding than weary. "Ellery wasn't about to attack me. He was trying to attack *himself*."

"Yeah," Ellery said. Seeing our shocked looks, he added, "Don't get me wrong. I'm not stupid enough to actually off myself or anything. I just figured if I cut myself up some, I'd have to leave school for a while. That way I could avoid the whole issue. Especially since I just found out after I planted that acid that Dr. Montgomery and the trustees have ordered the frats back in business starting tomorrow."

"What?" Darity blurted out, looking startled. "You must be mistaken. I didn't authorize any such thing."

"Well, you're not a Brother," Ellery sneered. "So I wouldn't expect you to know much."

"Enough, son," Marks barked out sharply. Then he turned and stormed off into the darkness.

"Hang on, Mr. Marks . . ." Darity took off after him.

Spencer and the other GTTers were sort of milling around, leaving me and Joe to continue questioning Ellery. He actually seemed calmer now that he'd said his piece. He even wandered over to Killer and gave him a pat.

That reminded me of something. "The dog attack," I said. "What was that about?"

"What dog attack?" Ellery rolled his eyes. "It never happened. I just wanted to get that nutty Hunt woman fired."

"Why?" Joe asked.

Ellery shrugged. "I was afraid she'd seen me messing with that fuse. Didn't want her to rat me out, so I faked the whole attack. Even paid off that Chip guy to play false witness, and made sure my mother heard about it so she'd get hysterical and call the school to make sure Hunt got fired."

I stared at the bandage on his arm. "So that's all for show?"

"Oh, no, there's a wound under there." Ellery pursed his lips and glanced at the knife I was still holding. "But I did it myself. Figured the small-town first aid kit they call a hospital up here would accept my story even if it didn't look quite like a real dog bite."

After that it wasn't difficult to get him to admit to most of the rest of the mischief. He confessed to helping spread those rumors about Darity wanting to shut down the frats, and to Spencer's recent "death threat." He'd also rigged the toilet bomb, though his face sort of crumpled when he admitted that part.

"I never meant for anyone to get really hurt," he said quietly. "I mean, a little shrapnel wound or whatever, sure. But not what happened to Lewis. I was planning to get in there first and stand back a bit so the explosion wouldn't hit anyone directly, you know?" He shot a look at the dog. "But Killer stopped me."

I couldn't help being shocked. Looking over at Joe, he looked the same. Even if Lewis's death was an accident, it was obvious that Ellery wasn't quite right in the head. Not if he was so willing to get himself and others hurt just to avoid dealing with his father.

He'd done the acid thing too. And also shot that arrow at Joe, though he claimed he wasn't really aiming for him—just trying to scare him and throw us off track.

The only incidents he wouldn't fess up to were

Lee's academic sabotage and the greased floor in the coach's office. He claimed to know nothing about either incident, aside from hearing about the latter like everyone else.

"Weird," Joe said as the two of us huddled to talk things over. "The grades thing could've been a computer glitch or something. But could the grease thing really be unrelated to all this?"

I kept a wary eye on Ellery. He was just standing there watching Killer, who was sniffing around at the edge of the clearing.

"I don't know," I said. "Might've been a team prank gone wrong, or maybe an innocent spill or something, I guess. We'll just have to leave that part to Dr. Darity to figure out."

Speaking of the headmaster, he'd just returned to the clearing, his expression troubled. Mr. Marks was behind him, glowering and looking generally mad at the world.

"Should we head back?" Spencer asked Darity, shooting a look at Ellery.

"I suppose we—," Darity began.

Killer drowned him out with several loud barks. I'd assumed he was taking a potty break over there at the edge of the clearing, but it seemed not. He took off into the woods, appearing to once more be on the track of something or someone.

"If he's just chasing a raccoon or something, I'm so not in the mood," Joe muttered as we both took off after him.

I put on a burst of speed. Whatever Killer was after, I was pretty sure it wasn't a raccoon.

We followed the dog through some underbrush and then along a faint, winding path. Soon we reached a smaller clearing. In it was another hunting cabin, this one older-looking and half falling down.

Killer raced straight over to it. "What is it, boy?" I asked, curious now.

Joe gulped as we caught up to the dog and saw what he had led us to. "Oh, wow," he said, playing his flashlight beam over something just inside the hut. "Is that what I think it is?"

Darity, Ellery, Spencer, and the others burst into the clearing behind us. "What is it?" Darity asked. "Why did the dog run away?"

Ellery hurried over to peer into the ramshackle cabin. "Ew, what's that?" he asked, looking mystified as he stared at two buckets brimming with some dark liquid.

Joe dipped his finger into one of the buckets and took a whiff. "Just as I thought," he said grimly. "It's blood. These are two buckets of blood."

I looked at Ellery and his father. They both

looked shocked and confused. And I was pretty sure that whatever else Ellery might be, he wasn't that good an actor.

Next I turned my gaze to Joe. He and I shared a long, serious look.

We might have landed one culprit. But it seemed that maybe the trouble at Firth Academy wasn't over after all.

Get ready to meet the next great kid detective,
Steve Brixton!

Here's an excerpt from *The* **BRIXTON BROTHERS**
Book #1: *The Case of the Case of
Mistaken Identity*

Steve Brixton, a.k.a. Steve, was reading on his too-small bed. He was having trouble getting comfortable, and for a few good reasons. His feet were hanging off the edge. Bedsprings were poking his ribs. His sheets were full of cinnamon-graham-cracker crumbs. But the main reason Steve was uncomfortable was that he was lying on an old copy of the *Guinness Book of World Records*, which was 959 pages long, and which he had hidden under his mattress.

If for some reason you were looking under Steve's mattress and found the *Guinness Book of World Records*, you'd probably think it was just an ordinary book. That was the point. Open it up and you'd see that Steve had cut an identical rectangle out from the middle of every one of its pages. Then he had pasted the pages together. It had taken over two weeks to finish, and Steve had developed an allergic reaction to the paste, but it was worth it. When Steve was done, the book had a secret compartment. It wasn't just a book anymore. It was a top secret book-box. And inside that top secret book-box was Steve's top secret notebook. And that top secret notebook was where Steve recorded all sorts of notes and observations, including, on page one, a list of the Fifty-Nine Greatest Books of All Time.

First on his list was a shiny red book called *The Bailey Brothers' Detective Handbook*, written by MacArthur Bart. The handbook was packed with the Real Crime-Solving Tips and Tricks employed by Shawn and Kevin Bailey, a.k.a. America's Favorite Teenage Supersleuths, a.k.a. the Bailey Brothers, in their never-ending fight against goons and baddies and criminals and crime. The Bailey Brothers, of course, were the heroes of the best detective stories of all time, the Bailey Brothers Mysteries. And their handbook told you everything they knew: what to look for at a crime scene (shoe prints, tire marks, and fingerprints), the ways to crack a safe (rip jobs, punch jobs, and old man jobs), and where to hide a top secret notebook (in a top secret book-box). Basically, *The Bailey Brothers' Detective Handbook* told you how to do all the stuff that the Bailey Brothers were completely ace at.

The Bailey Brothers, of course, were the sons of world-famous detective Harris Bailey. They helped their dad solve his toughest cases, and they had all sorts of dangerous adventures, and these adventures were the subject of the fifty-eight shiny red volumes that made up the Bailey Brothers Mysteries, also written by MacArthur Bart. Numbers two through fifty-nine on Steve Brixton's list of the Fifty-Nine Greatest Books of All Time were taken up by the Bailey Brothers Mysteries.

Steve had already read all the Bailey Brothers books. Most of them he had read twice. A few he'd read three times. His favorite Bailey Brothers mystery was whichever one he was reading at the time. That meant that right now, as Steve lay on his lumpy bed, his favorite book was Bailey Brothers #13: *The Mystery of the Hidden Secret*. Steve was finishing up chapter seventeen, which at the moment was his favorite chapter, and which ended like this:

"Jumping jackals!" dark-haired Shawn exclaimed, pointing to the back wall of the dusty old parlor. "Look, Kevin! That bookcase looks newer than the rest!"

"General George Washington!" his blond older brother cried out. "I think you're right!" Kevin rubbed his chin and thought. "Hold on just a minute, Shawn. This mansion has been abandoned for years. Nobody lives here. So who would have built a new bookshelf?"

Shawn and Kevin grinned at each other. "The robbers!" they shouted in unison.

"Say, I'll bet this bookshelf covers a secret passageway that leads to their hideout," Shawn surmised.

"Which is where we'll find the suitcase full of stolen loot!" Kevin cried.

The two sleuths crossed over to the wall and stood in front of the suspicious bookcase. Shawn thought quietly for a few seconds.

"I know! Let's try to push the bookcase over," Shawn suggested.

"Hey, it can't be any harder than Coach Biltmore's tackling practice," joked athletic Kevin, who lettered in football and many other varsity sports.

"One, two, three, heave!" shouted Shawn. The boys threw their weight into the bookshelf, lifting with their legs to avoid back injuries. There was a loud crash as the bookshelf detached from the wall and toppled over. The dust cleared and revealed a long, dark hallway!

"I knew it!" whooped Shawn. "Let's go!"

"Not so fast, kids," said a strange voice. "You won't be recoverin' the loot that easy."

Shawn and Kevin whirled around to see a shifty-eyed man limping toward them, his scarred face visible in the moonlight through the window.

The man was holding a knife!

That was where the chapter ended, and when Carol Brixton, a.k.a. Steve's mom, called him downstairs to dinner.

THE HARDY BOYS

THE PERFECT CRIME

Play Frank and Joe in an all-new VIDEO GAME!

Available April 2009.
www.hardyboysgames.com

FRANKLIN W. DIXON

THE HARDY BOYS

Undercover Brothers®

INVESTIGATE THESE TWO ADVENTUROUS MYSTERY TRILOGIES WITH AGENTS FRANK AND JOE HARDY!

#25 Double Trouble

#26 Double Down

#28 Galaxy X

#29 X-plosion

#27 Double Deception

#30 The X-Factor

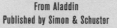
From Aladdin
Published by Simon & Schuster

CURL UP WITH A GOOD MYSTERY!

From Aladdin
Published by Simon & Schuster

CHECK OUT SOME OTHER GHOSTLY BOOKS FROM ALADDIN: